The Black Widow

By The International Writers
for Justice

The International Writers for Justice

List of Authors

Mark Kodama

Garrison McKnight

Kathryn Meyer

Jim Bates

L.T, Waterson

P.C. Darkcliff

Angelika Delf

Chris Irons

Jan Emslie

Maria Jesu Estraada

Bernice Groves

Heather Hood

Jill Kiesow

Silvana McGuire

David Montoya

Nerisha Kemraj

Rich Rurshell

Table of Contents

The Black Widow

Part I.

Chapter 1

By Mark Kodama and Heather Hood

Big John met her in a Vegas nightclub as she danced underneath the strobe light, her toned body trying to burst from the tight clothes that hugged her hips. She closed her eyes, and put her hands behind her head as she gyrated to the music. She laughed playfully blowing her blond hair from her face as others danced around her. She could feel the young men staring at her in lust.

The huge man in the front of her flashed his Rolex at her. *That must be him*, she thought. This would be easy. Big John asked her to dance. There was not much to Big John but women were attracted to his handsome face and powerful body. He regularly worked out at the gym when he was not clubbing.

"Sure," she smiled, making sure he saw her look him up and down. The acrid, pungent smell of sweat, not completely covered by her expensive perfume, filled the air as sweat ran down her face. The smell did not bother him at all. Indeed, it turned him on. She held out her right hand. "Erika," she said.

He reached for her hand and shook it. Though it was hot in the club her hand was ice cold.

"John," he replied.

She reached into her purse and took out a small mirror. She touched up her feathered hair and put on additional lipstick and then smiled, pressing her lips together.

He kissed her black widow tattoo on her right shoulder. She had a birthmark like gunshot wound next to the tattoo. When she smiled, her black eyes sparkled. Her eyes said "I want you."

"Let's get out of here," Erika said.

"Where to?"

"More comfortable environs," she said.

He took her to his house just outside of town. It was a nice house that his mother purchased for him after he graduated from college.

When they got inside his doorway, she pressed against him, and slid a hand leisurely down his stomach, reaching for his pants. He involuntarily groaned. He began to kiss her furiously, pulling her blouse and bra off.

When he reached down her pants, she breathed in his ear, "Not yet."

"What?" he panted.

"I need another drink."

"What will you have?"

"A Jack and Ginger - no ice."

Big John made Erika a drink at the bar as she looked out at his swimming pool in his backyard.

"Let's go for a swim," she said.

"I only have swim trunks for myself."

"We won't need them," she said with a wicked grin.

Big John watched the rest of her clothes fall to her feet before she ran laughing to the swimming pool and dove naked into the water. Big John rifled through her clothes, finding a business card for the Blue Moon Strip Club. He set the card on the table. Oh, yeah, this one would be coming back.

When Big John saw Erika swimming naked in his pool, her perfectly tan skin glistening under the full moon, he knew he finally had her.

Although he'd had a couple of drinks, his head was clear as he dove into the cold water and swam to her. The chlorine was a little strong. He would mention that to Pedro when he came to clean the pool in the morning.

Erika's dark eyes shone with delight and her lips broke into a wide smile. He caught her leg as she tried to swim away.

When she turned and shoved the knife between his ribs, he never saw it coming. Tendrils of blood flowed from his body into the pool like a crimson spider web as he sank under the water.

Chapter 2

By Garrison McKnight

Big John was still blowing bubbles at the bottom of the pool as Erika calmly washed the blood off the knife.

Avoiding the stair rail so she wouldn't leave any fingertips, she lifted herself out of the pool, dressed, then moved on to the tedious task of wiping Big John's place of her fingerprints – mainly the wall at the entrance where her palms touched when Big John pushed her for a kiss.

Donning latex gloves, she turned over furniture, vases, opened drawers, making a mess in the living room. Big John's wallet was still in his pants; she pocketed his money. Davenport hired her to do this job and paid her good money, but if she was found out, the amount he paid her wouldn't go far; it would barely get her out of the country. She dropped the credit cards and business cards on the floor – Golden Domes, The Frisky Pussy Cat, Svetlana's Girls. Big John sure got around. Erika grabbed the Rolex and dropped it into her bag. She checked on the pool again, satisfied that Big John was not coming back up for air.

Slipping out through the back gate, Erika returned to the car she'd left a few blocks from John's earlier that day.

***

Erika was a crowd pleaser at the Blue Moon, one of the most upmarket strip clubs in downtown Las Vegas. Stripping was one of her many cover jobs. Some days she taught yoga; other days she was a personal trainer at the local gym, a cocktail hostess, a croupier at a gaming table. She worked many different jobs to get close to her marks and the IRS. Stripping was the job she liked least, but it made her less than stellar clients feel "safe."

It was nearly midnight when she strolled into the pounding music of the crowded strip bar, brushing past the men sitting at a table on "perve row" ogling Bouncing Betty gyrating around the pole, never noticing the woman in street clothes who'd just entered the bar. Erika was glad for the distraction. The men were lined up at the foot of the stage to shove dollar bills into the black lace garter belt of the well-endowed strip tease artist. Betty was not a particularly good dancer but then again she did not need to be. Erika ducked out of sight hiding the knife in the toilet tank of the stripper's private restroom.

Sporting the "Fetish Fishnet Teddy" and a red bob in place of her black mane, "Tiger Lily" walked out on stage to wolf whistles and catcalls. They couldn't get enough of the Asian siren from the Philippines.

***

It was 2 a.m. when Erika made it home. She slipped out of her jeans to be a little more comfortable. It was then she realized she no longer had the business card of The Blue Moon where she worked as a cover. *Damn. Big John probably filched it from my pocket. I may have to go back.*

Opening the refrigerator door, she bent down to see what she had to eat. Nothing like a good old-fashioned murder to make you hungry. Not much there.

A man came up from behind and covered her mouth.

Chapter 3
By Jill Kiesow

W ithout hesitation, Erika threw an elbow up and out behind her, catching her attacker in the mouth, giving her just enough distance to turn and knee him square in the groin.

Only when she heard the expletives in the charming British accent did she pause – fingers in midair ready to gouge flesh – and look at him in the face.

"Davenport!" She helped him straighten himself and tried to smooth the wrinkles in his expensive suit. "What the hell are you doing here?"

"Apparently getting worked over by one of the best assassins I've ever hired."

Erika dabbed his mouth with a cloth napkin from the dining room table and apologized.

"Entirely my fault, dear. I should have known better than to try to have a little fun with you."

She motioned him to the couch while she got him a scotch on the rocks.

"You did an exceptional job with Big John," he said.

"It was nothing."

"It was quite something darling. I wasn't let down by my high expectations. Couldn't have played him better if you had him on strings."

When Erika sat beside him, Davenport leaned back and caressed her black widow tattoo. "The rumors I heard about your skill were true," he said. "Nice tattoo." He moved his mouth to her skin and murmured the last.

"My tattoo is part of me, it marks me. This is who I am, whether I like it or not, a member of the Black Widows."

"Do you like it?"

"I do. Not that it really matters. It pays well. A girl has to take care of herself."

Straightening, Davenport sipped his drink. "That, I know. You've heard about my mother?"

"We all have. The original Black Widow. She's a legend."

"You remind me of her."

"She took care of herself and many others," he laughed. "Now there was a woman with skill."

"Knocking off big, dumb guys like the one tonight isn't that hard. Covering your trail, now that can be a challenge. I nailed it though. I even found a good spot for the knife. I can retrieve it later."

"It's not worth anything, love. But tell me…were you able to recover the item?"

"Yeah, I got the Rolex. It's fake. He didn't have much of value in that whole ostentatious place." She reached into her purse and dropped the watch in his lap. "You've got your planes and cars and casino. What did you want that ugly thing for?"

Quickly, Davenport slid the watch into his breast pocket, patted it lovingly, drained his drink, and stood to go. "Oh, Erika, darling. That cheap watch is now the most valuable thing I own."

Chapter 4

By Mark Kodama

When Pedro arrived at Big John's house at 10 a.m. sharp, he was really annoyed. If Johnny was not Detective Wallace's son, he would have terminated his account long ago. Pedro slipped on his latex gloves and picked up the empty beer cans on the front lawn and then threw them in the recycling bin. When he opened the lid, he found used condoms on top of the recyclables

"Pendejo!"

Looking up to the sun, Pedro held his right hand against his right eyebrow, shading his eyes. Although it was morning, it was nearly 100 degrees. Today was going to be a scorcher.

Detective Wallace was a man of integrity and principle, a man for whom Pedro would do anything. Johnny was a spoiled kid. Detective Wallace's biggest weakness was he loved his son too much.

Pedro hoped Johnny was not home. He did not want to listen to Johnny's drivel about how much he liked "chicas" and Taco Bell. He could see him now sunning himself on a lounge chair wearing his mirrored aviator sunglasses and his crimson "Make America Great Again" baseball cap.

"One of these days, someone was going to let Johnny have it," Pedro said to himself. Pedro unloaded his cleaning tools and hoses from the bed of his white pick up and carried them to the house.

He opened the latch on the back gate and walked to the pool. His mouth dropped open when he saw a naked man floating face down in the pool.

Pedro called 911.

Chapter 5

By David K. Montoya

Blue and red lights had danced in the coin-colored sky for almost an hour when the crime scene officers heard the backfire of Bruce Wallace's old Plymouth. Puck-e-ta . . .puck-et-a . . . puck-et-ka. The worn-out old vehicle was always breaking down. Det. Wallace could hear the tires scrape against metal as he turned, pulling into the familiar driveway.

With his shock of white hair, dressed in brown polyester pants and an old manila shirt with a frayed collar, Wallace exited moments later. He was met **by** multiple uniformed officers; some he knew but most he did not. They all wore an unmistakable mask of concern. Det. Wallace was legendary for solving near impossible crime cases and so was his temper.

"Detective Wallace…"

"Where is he…? Where's my son?"

"I will have one of the guys walk you to the pool area," an officer stammered.

"I helped Johnny dig the hole for that damned pool. I know *exactly* where it's at! Is that where I'll find him?" His voice raised to a higher pitch. "Is that where I will find my son?"

The officer nodded.

Wallace made a beeline for the back gate which led into the poolside area. His stomach knotted with the thought of his ex-wife. How will Edna react when she is told? Then he saw the water stained with his son's blood.

"Oh, Johnny what have you done!?"

Wallace walked over to the edge of the pool. The blood-drained corpse of his boy still floated atop the water. "Jesus Christ! People! Somebody get my boy out of there!"

Despite Wallace's legendary poker face, uncontrollable tears fell. A flash of memories followed: holding John in the hospital as a newborn, a birthday that he was actually there for, the time he graduated high school. Edna had really taken him to the cleaners in their divorce settlement, even if she always made more money than he did. She bought this house for her and Johnny, and then moved to her upscale condo.

With a sigh, Wallace wiped away his tears with the sleeves of his light jacket. *I'm sorry, Johnny. I will find out who did this to you!*

"Detective Wallace..." Whick extended his hand.

"Whick..."

Wallace heaved one more sigh and shook his hand. "Thank you, Sergeant."

"Do you know who would want to do this?" the younger man asked.

Wallace looked around the scene. "I've made more than a few enemies over the years."

"Do you think it was a mafia hit?"

"This was a professional hit, Sergeant. And it was a woman who did it."

"A woman?" Whick questioned. "With all due respect, sir, your son was six-foot-three and almost three hundred pounds of muscle. This also was a robbery. There's no way a woman could..."

"Johnny was naked, Sergeant. I've never known for someone to drop their clothes at the door and jump into the pool alone."

Wallace stood in silence as he watched the men load his son's dead body into a body bag, until something caught his eye.

"Wait! Wait! Don't zip it up yet!"

The officers paused and waited for the older detective to trot over to them.

"Hold up his left arm," Wallace ordered.

They lifted Big John's left arm. He had a tan line from always wearing a watch.

"Where is his watch? Did someone see his watch?"

Chapter 6

By Mark Kodama

When Edna McFarland Wallace received a phone call from the Las Vegas Metropolitan Police Department, Homicide Division, she felt mostly anger. She remembered the words of her father, Old Man McFarland: "There will be plenty of time for tears later."

"Jenny! Jenny!" She shouted into her speaker.

Where the hell is she!

Looking at the view from her corner office in the ten-story George Washington Center, her lips tensed. *I knew that fool would get himself into trouble someday.*

If only she'd never married that good for nothing, then she would have never had to raise her less-than-nothing son. If only she'd had a daughter.

She called her ex-husband, let it ring two times and then it shut off. She dialled it again. And again nothing.

"Jenny!" *God, where is that idiot?*

"Yes, Ms. McFarland?" Jenny hurriedly entered the office, explaining, "There was a situation with a plaintiff lawyer..."

"I don't care. I eat plaintiff lawyers for breakfast! I'm going to have to take the day off. If something *important* comes up, reach me on my cell."

Edna was a larger than life personality. One of the best insurance defence lawyers in the city; tough as nails and sharp as a whip. When an insurance company had a difficult high dollar case, they called Edna. And she was worth every penny of what she was paid.

"Where are you going... if anyone asks?"

"To find my good-for-nothing ex-husband. And when I find him, I'm going to break him in two."

Chapter 7
By Jim Bates

Wallace's office was separated from the cops in the bullpen area by clear Plexiglas windows and a door that was always open. But that didn't matter today because Wallace was in a daze, sitting slumped at his desk, a shell of the man he used to be. Sure, he was a seasoned detective, but it was all too much. He rubbed his hands over his face, feeling the exhaustion of the last few days in rough, three-day-old beard stubble. He wasn't eating, he wasn't sleeping, he was drinking too much. His stale body odor filled the room.

Now this. He stared at the three- ring binder on his desk. The Murder Book. It's what he and everyone else on the force involved in the case would use to file documents, notes and whatever else was pertinent to the case. When they found Johnny's killer, the binder would be bulging. Wallace hoped so, anyway. To his way of thinking, the more information they were able to find, the faster they'd track down the person or persons responsible for killing his son. He knew it in his gut, though, there was more than one.

He caressed the binder and took a deep breath and opened it, starting to feel more like himself. At least he was doing something. He forced himself to focus. The last thing in his life he ever expected to do was solve his son's murder. But he was ready. It's what he did. He was a detective.

The first items of interest were the business cards found on the floor at Johnny's place. Svetlana's Girls, the Golden Domes and a number of other clubs. He turned around and looked out into the bullpen. Where the hell was Whick? He'd need him to help with interviews.

When he didn't immediately see the younger sergeant, he turned back to the binder and looked at the cards again. Three places to check out. Toss in for good measure the nearly one-hundred casinos, bars and dance clubs in Vegas, and you had a big job ahead. Had anyone seen Big John on the night of his murder? Somebody needed to check his cell phone records to see where he may have been.

Questions asked. Hard questions. What would he find about his son he didn't already know? That he didn't *want* to know? There wasn't any evidence of drugs of any kind. And his blood alcohol was under the legal limit. Wallace took a deep breath to calm down. He thought of his son's last moments: the crimson clouds hovering in the water, seared forever in his memory. Never to be forgotten.

He picked up the first crime scene photo. It showed Johnny's abdomen and a small hole under the third rib. Then he looked at a photo of the same wound taken during autopsy. Just one stab wound. The report confirmed his suspicions: it was a knife wound that had pierced Johnny's heart, the kind of killing wound only performed by someone who knew what they were doing. A professional.

There was a knock at his office doorway and Wallace looked up to see Sergeant Whick standing there, nervously shifting his feet back and forth like he had to go to the restroom.

"God damn it, Whick. Where the hell have you been?"

"Sorry, sir," the mild-mannered sergeant stammered. "I went over to the lab to get the pool water analysis. They found something interesting and I thought you'd like to see it right away." He waved a folder. "It's what they found in the pool filter. It's pretty interesting…"

"Hand it over now. Let's see it."

Wallace yanked the folder out of Whick's hand.

"You get a chance to look at it?"

"Yeah, I did. I thought you might be pleased."

A surge of energy rushed through Wallace. "What is it?" God only knew he could go for some good news.

"Take a look. Look what they found in the pool filter."

Wallace read out loud, "Blond hair. Straight. Twelve inches long." He looked at Whick and slammed his hand on the desk. Bam! "Know what this means?" Whick shook his head to the negative. Wallace leaned forward, "It means we're looking for a blonde. Likely a woman with long blond hair. We need a DNA test."

His exhaustion melted away like ice in a whiskey glass. "We've got to start checking bars and casinos. Right now. We're looking for a woman with shoulder length hair like in the filter, a natural blonde." He got to his feet. "Let's go."

"Where do you think you're going?" *Fucking lieutenant motherfucking Dense*, leaning on the doorframe. "You're in no shape to conduct an investigation, Wallace."

Chapter 8
By Jan Emslie

They all thought they knew Davenport. Borderline psychopath with flame red hair and a temper to match. Seared into his memory was the indignation of being turned away from their gang, then standing on the outside while they divided up their shares. He could still hear them laughing as he cried all the way home where his mother took a backhander across his right cheek. The first and only time she'd struck him.

Running the exclusive triple AAA escort service Svetlana's Girls, three-Legged Dan was a mere facade. Those "in the know" and who could afford it, knew it was one of Davenport's operations. Nothing was too much trouble. A substantial amount of cash could buy you your heart's desire and more.

Davenport never married, never had the need when he had the pick of the candy store. His mother was right on three counts: she was the only woman he'd ever need, he that controls the women holds the power, and never let anyone humiliate you. To that he'd add: don't be rash and savor the hurt until it's an exploding rage in your chest, then wait until they have something worth talking, something that will burn their soul, like money . . . a child . . . a wife . . . a pretty daughter perhaps? Then strike.

The high-pitched shrill of his office phone brought him back to reality; tiny specs of saliva hung from the corners of his mouth like a hungry dog. He inspected the caller ID. Ah, good. All business was personal and the most important of his clients needed to feel special.

"Yes, tell Mr. Orange I have the girls here for him," Davenport said into the telephone. "Two Russian girls and one Slovenian. Golden showers are not a problem, sir, but you do know it's a thousand extra per girl. No, we don't have any hidden cameras. We are strictly professional."

He listened for a moment and then replied, "That's great. I will pencil in Mr. Orange for the 4th of July. My airstrip is at his disposal. Take care. See you soon."

Closing his leather-bound diary, he slipped the gold pen back in his pocket and let his thoughts return to the next victim Roman Santini. *Hate that guy. Where ever I turn he is in my face. Thinks he's a big shot.*

Davenport had a busy day ahead of him. He spoke into his hand-held recorder, "I've a kidnapping and a wedding to fix. I must check the stock market. I've also a funeral to prepare for. . . ."

Chapter 9

By Rich Rurshell

Davenport poured himself another whiskey and walked across the study to the high-backed chair at his desk. He slumped down into it and took a sip of his drink before reaching into his jacket pocket and pulling out Big John's watch. Although it was scorching hot outside, the air conditioning in the building made it chilly inside. Inserting homing and listening devices into the watch was sheer genius. He picked up the picture frame he kept of his late mother on his desk.

As he turned it over, he noticed movement in his peripheral vision. He looked towards the window to see a tall, thin man standing in the light. Davenport pulled open his drawer and took out his Colt Mustang.

"And who exactly are you?" he asked, pointing the gun at the man by the window. The man just smiled.

"Am I amusing you? You won't find it too funny when I put a bullet through your brain."

"You might struggle to shoot me without any bullets in your gun, Mr. Davenport," replied the man, eyes still locked on Davenport's, grin still firmly in place. He held up the clip from Davenport's gun.

Davenport realized immediately from the weight of his gun that the man before him was indeed holding his clip.

"What do you want?"

"I'm surprised you haven't you haven't figured it out yet, Mr. Davenport. You asked Tarver to send you the best, and I am the best."

"You're Tarver's new break-in chap!" said Davenport, putting the gun down on his desk, a smile creeping upon his face. "You're very good! How did you get past my security?"

"For the right fee, I could tell you how to make your home impenetrable," said the man, tossing the clip to Davenport. "But that is not why I am here. Tarver tells me you need me to plant something in Big John Wallace's house. I am here to get it."

"Right down to business. I like it. Here…" Davenport held out the watch to the man. "Mister. . ?"

"Dedos is sufficient for now, Mr. Davenport." The man took the watch and pocketed it without looking at it.

"You know, Big John may have pretty high-tech security at…"

"It's nothing," interrupted the man. "I've already been inside. Who do you think installed it?" He reached into his pocket and threw something onto the desk in front of Davenport. "A gift."

Davenport looked down at the red "Boss" underwear lying before him. "Big John Wallace's?"

The man nodded.

"When Tarver told me what you'd cost I was a little taken aback, but you're good. You're really very good indeed."

"The best," replied the man, grinning again.

"Let me or Tarver know when the job is done, and I'll wire Tarver the rest of your money."

"Fine. I'd only come and take it if you didn't."

"Maybe once the job is done, we can discuss those improvements to my security you spoke about."

"After we've settled the fee."

"Of course."

"Then alert security that I will be coming through the house. I'm leaving through the front door."

"Certainly." Davenport picked up his phone and called his head of security. "Jimmy, tell your men to pay no attention to the gentleman dressed in black heading out of the house. They shouldn't find that difficult since he managed to get to my office unchallenged. You're lucky I'm in a good mood, and he wasn't here to assassinate me." He put the phone back down on the desk.

"Thanks, Mr. Davenport. Have a great day." The man disappeared through the door without making a sound.

Davenport sat back in his chair. The next part of his plan was now in motion. *I will have my revenge.*

Chapter 10
By Jan Emslie

Taking in his fine art collection, the Caravaggio on the rosewood Chippendale, Davenport smiled. Women were deadlier than men and he'd been taught by the best. Men always needed "something" and the antidote to "want" was seduction. A sure fire way of leaving a man salivating for more was by giving him just less than enough. Davenport preferred hiring women. Red, Jane, Heidi, Erika and the rest of the Black Widows. They'd never let him down and were easy on the eye, if not on the pocket.

He pressed a button and Vivaldi's Concerto Number 4 in F minor filled the room. Instinctively he closed his eyes and tapped his finger on the armrest in time to the music.

His mother Stella started as a grifter, playing the numbers and then worked her way up to working as an international assassin. No one got in her way, least of all his father. One bruised lip too many and he watched as Daddy cascaded down the stairs, tipped by the point of a well-aimed stiletto, vertebrae cracking as he hit each step, dead before he hit the bottom. His mother was the original black widow. Perhaps his deep brown eyes and thirst for finer things wasn't all he'd inherited from her. No one stood in his way either.

Davenport would use Erika for the next kill. With her coldness, she could crack a man's head like a chestnut with her thighs and was a poet with a whip. Translucent skin and blond hair straight from the catwalk. He made sure all the girls had legitimate days jobs leaving room for night time misandry.

Davenport pictured Big John dead, fighting a lungful of pool water and a stab wound to the heart. He exhaled while Vivaldi reached a crescendo. He thought of Wallace and his son Big John. He smiled.

Davenport picked Roman Santini next. He knew his weakness, flattery and blondes. Davenport was nothing but thorough, having his men go through the trash, watching the goings and comings of the next kill. It would be done right.

Santini hated heights but would meet a beautiful woman on the top of the Stratosphere Casino if he thought it would bring in a few thousand bucks. No one challenged Davenport without paying a price.

He smiled as he made the call. When she picked up he commanded, "Erika, a car will be with you in ten. Stop what you're doing."

Chapter 11

By Heather Hood

Something about the face in the photographs of 'Roman Santini' was

familiar. Erika knew it; she just couldn't quite remember.

She kept to the shadows of the entrance way, studying the man in the picture provided by Davenport. Good looks, wavy brown hair, slim, muscular build. His face didn't fit her memories, and yet…the body language. The way he moved. She checked the toggle on her bracelet, making sure the silk was loose. Poison would have been better, but with security cameras everywhere, his death would have to look like an accident. High above, the observation deck rotated.

Heads turned when she entered the restaurant. They always did. She was used to it. Jealous women and their drooling men. Her hips swayed a little in silent acknowledgment of their regard, enjoying the attention, like a cat teasing a dog on the other side of a sliding glass door. Roman turned and smiled, presenting a perfect red rose, with a small bow. Davenport must have told him she liked roses.

"Mr. Santini, party of two?" The hostess asked, motioning toward a dimly-lit table set slightly back from the others, toward the rear wall. A bottle of Champagne chilled in a silver bucket beside the table.

Roman held her chair, then slid into his own. A waiter hovered, anxious to pour the champagne for Santini's approval. Once he nodded, her glass was filled and Santini held up his for a toast.

"To old friends," he said, with a smile.

The moment she heard his voice she *knew*. She would know that British accent if it came out of a howling Antarctic windstorm.

"I said I'd kill you if I ever saw you again," Erika said.

"Is that any way to greet the one who made you who you are?"

"My hard work made me who I am. You just took all the credit."

Four years of hell worse than any special ops boot camp at the hands of the man only known as 'Ghost.' Or G. Hudson. They were the only names by which she knew him. She'd learned fast, then beaten him senseless one night and ran to America. That explained the unrecognizable face.

"As I remember, you were dying when I picked you up off the street. I taught you how to survive." The clipped words betrayed no irritation at all. Another one of his games.

Don't let his head games get to you. Do the job and get out. Except the job had taken an unexpected twist, now. Implied sex was out of the question. She would need another angle.

"As I recall, you were dying when I left."

His smile stretched into something feral, his voice became a vicious whisper, "You should have made sure I was dead."

She took a swallow of champagne, letting the bubbles tickle their way down her throat and laughed.

"But then we wouldn't be having this lovely dinner tonight, now would we? Why are you here Hudson? Or am I supposed to call you Roman now?"

He waved an immaculately manicured hand in dismissal, as if it didn't interest him. "What did Davenport tell you about me?"

"I don't know what you are talking about."

One of his eyes twitched at the choice of words. "Well," he said leaning forward and placing his hands on the table, "I think we both know that's not how stories really work."

***

Once upon a time they had been closer than lovers. She had to remember that as she watched his hands move in familiar patterns that brought back memories of his flesh pressed against hers. Those hands had moved up her back just like that. Everyone else had a past, she thought with a hint of icy acceptance. Hers lay shallowly buried. Her story was trust no one.

Like the other Black Widow here tonight, for instance, who was so obviously reading their lips. What was she doing here? The more she thought about it, the more she became convinced Davenport didn't trust her. Or was it the Ghost? Could Davenport possibly know about their history?

Roman spun dinner conversations about his successful underworld operations until the dishes were cleared, leaving her to plan the next move. If Davenport did not trust her again it was time to think about moving on. With her skills she wouldn't have to worry about employment. But there was a little matter of the job at hand.

"We need to get some air," she smiled, cutting her eyes toward the hostess. He understood. "All that champagne went straight to my head."

"Might I suggest a walk on the observation deck?" He stood and offered her his arm.

Ah, Ghost. How I'll miss you once I kill you again.

"What happened to the unicorn?" She asked once the elevator door closed.

He pulled a gold chain out from his shirt. A cheap child's ring dangled from it. "Not something you can wear openly, I'm afraid."

"How is she?"

"I've no idea. She thinks I'm dead."

"Lots of children grow up without parents."

"Erika..."

The door opened with a slight swoosh of cooler air. "No." she said, building a wall of ice between them. Long powerful legs carried her out into the night.

"Do you hate her that much?" he asked, following her out into the night. "I never pegged you for one of those heartless women who would toss a child..."

She slapped him hard across the face. She could have broken his cheekbones again, but something stopped her. Maybe it was the echo of his voice in Chiani's laughter. Well, he would never hear it, she would make sure of that tonight.

"Is this the part where you kill me?"

He backed to the elevator door, his steps silent despite his size. He lacked the unconscious grace of his youth, she noticed. Either she had really damaged him, or life had treated him badly. That face: he had paid a lot of money to have it changed, but she couldn't say it looked better.

He ran his hands through his hair in a gesture so unfamiliar she stared. "Don't you ever get tired?"

"No. I love what I do."

She noted he knew better than to get within striking distance. He kept his arms loose.

"What if I told you there was a way to use what I taught you to make things right for those who can't. Just name your price. Would you at least hear me out?"

"Start talking," she sauntered forward, unwinding the silk snare from her bracelet.

"Crooked judges and corrupt politicians. All under Davenport's thumb. Help me take him down. "

"What's the catch?" She looped the silk over her hands, testing its strength.

"Well," he shrugged, and grinned that little sideways grin of his. "We would have to become lovers again. Or at least look like it."

She started to laugh. After a moment, his nervous laughter joined hers. The snare fell into the shadows at their feet as their arms wound around each other. Just another job, she thought, and if she could name her own price... Chiara would love Italy this time of year.

Chapter 12

By L.T. Waterson

"What is this supposed to be?" Davenport peered with exaggerated horror into the cup he was holding.

"It's the tea you asked for."

Davenport sighed. He should have known better than to ask Susie to fetch his tea. Over many patient days his housekeeper had learned just how Davenport liked this particular beverage but, alas, the woman had called in sick this morning, offering up her daughter as a substitute.

"It'll just be for the day."

She then proceeded to tell him exactly how bad she felt but he had filtered her out. James Davenport was far too busy to attend to female wittering.

"Take it away." He passed the cup back to the girl. What was her name again? Samantha, Susie . . . something like that.

She seemed to panic. Good housekeepers were as rare as hen's teeth and sometimes it behooved a man to turn a blind eye.

Davenport stood up and strode across the room. Perhaps some music was called for. Wagner.

A ping from the laptop sitting on a table by the large picture window caught his attention. With a frown he killed the music. It was

his favourite part as well, Siegfried on his way to face the dragon
Fafnir.

The email was from one of his eyes and ears and consisted of
a three-word message, 'Look at this'.

There were video files attached to the email. As Davenport
selected the first of the files a cold sensation flooded his stomach.

It was obviously CCTV footage. The images were a little
blurred, and leeched of any color or sound they reminded him of the
old black and white films that he had watched during his time at Eton.

The first showed a man and woman. They were arm in arm,
the woman clearly giggling and leaning on the man. He watched as the
pair disappeared into the building. It was obviously Erika and Santini.
He had already noted the time stamp and there was no mistaking
Erika's willowy height or the breadth of Santini's shoulders.

Davenport moved on to the second file. This one showed him
Erika emerging from the building alone. He checked the time stamp. In
just a couple of minutes he would be standing by his car, eager to know
if his enemy was dead.

Why three, though? Davenport hated suspense and he loathed
not knowing. His hand shook as he opened the last file.

The counter in the corner displayed a time that was a few
minutes prior to Erika's departure. As Davenport watched, a man
emerged from the revolving doorway and walked quickly past the
camera and away. His head was bowed and his face obscured, but
Davenport knew those broad shoulders of Roman Santini.

Chapter 13

By Mark Kodama

Dedos pulled up in his ten-year-old Japanese compact. He certainly could afford a nicer car bought and paid by the tax-free money he made as a professional burglar, but he needed to blend into the crowd, hide in the shadows – become invisible in plain sight. He parked a block away from Big John's house. He put on his leather gloves and fanny pack with the tools he needed to get into the house. He opened the fanny pack, again checking that he had Big John's gold watch with Davenport's homing and listening devices installed inside.

He looked at his watch with his penlight. 2 a.m. He turned off his cell phone and then hid it underneath the driver's side car seat. He walked quickly and silently forward as if he lived in the neighborhood. He wore dark slacks and a black turtle neck sweater. He kept his eyes forward watching his left and his right through his peripheral vision.

Big John's house was in a quiet middle class neighborhood. Nevada is the only state he knew of where prostitution was legal except for Clark County. But the state also seemed to have more churches per person than any other place that he knew.

Dedos silently opened the back gate and slipped into the backyard. He had checked the layout on Google Earth and in the county records. He slipped through the side door into the garage. All was quiet. He put his ear against the door leading to the house. Silence.

He quietly opened the door and then slipped inside. He looked for a conspicuous place to leave the watch, somewhere Wallace will find it. Ah, the kitchen table. He aimed his penlight on the kitchen table. There was a business card on the table. Some strip joint. Figures. Davenport had briefed him on Big John.

Suddenly, Dedos felt someone grab him in a choke hold from behind, covering his mouth at the same time. He felt a vise grip around his neck, powerful. It was strange. He smelled the hint of ladies perfume. He could feel himself getting weak and light headed

He had to do something or he would die.

Chapter 14

By- Mark Kodama

It wasn't long before Det. Wallace received a call from Whick.

Although it was morning, a mass of reporters gathered like a swarm of flies outside of the police tape surrounding John's property. Half a dozen police vehicles, including the forensic team, were parked in front of the house. Two murders in one week. Which told him the new body was a man who was dressed like a cat burglar. The coroner pulled up in his vehicle.

"Hey, Bruce," the coroner said grimly.

'Dr. Klimek," Wallace replied.

Bruce and Dr. Klimek walked by the police officers standing outside and crossed under the police tape, bending and lifting the tape all in one motion.

"Detective Wallace. Detective Wallace," the reporters brayed.

"Have you identified the second victim?" asked one.

"Were your son and the new victim lovers?" asked another.

"Sorry… No questions," Wallace said.

"How does it feel that your son is dead?" another reporter asked.

"Vultures," Dr. Klimek grumbled.

When they entered the front door, a dozen police officers were milling about collecting evidence. One of them was inspecting the wire where the alarm sensor used to be in the entrance hall. Sgt. Whick greeted them at the door.

"Detective Wallace. Dr. Klimek."

"Let's get to it," Wallace said.

"Hispanic man. About thirty. Dressed in a black turtle neck, dark slacks. Possibly strangled."

"Know who he is?'

"Not yet."

His face seemed familiar to Wallace.

"Do you know who he is?" The doctor could see Wallace's reaction.

"Face is familiar." Wallace looked around. Johnny's gold watch was on the table. It was certainly not there before.

"Dust the table and look for fingerprints." The forensic team put the watch in a clear plastic bag and marked it as evidence.

Lt. Dense was eating a baloney sandwich. His favorite blue tie stained with the mustard of many baseball games did not reach the black leather belt holding up his hiked-up brown polyester pants.

"Wallace," Dense said.

"Lieutenant."

"Boy, your son sure had some interesting acquaintances," Dense smirked, biting into his sandwich and hiking up his pants with his free hand.

Wallace felt his jaw tighten.

"My police intuition says these murders were done by a white man – a serial killer," Lt. Dense said, chewing loudly. "I have a sixth sense for this kind of thing."

"We have a female killer" Wallace said. "I know my son. He had a thing for the ladies. You at least should leave open the possibility that our suspect is a woman."

"You are wrong, wrong, wrong, Wallace," Lt. Dense said. "How could a woman kill a hulk like your son? Impossible. The whole skinny dipping thing is a hoax to mislead us."

"I think you know I've cracked some of the hardest cases this city has ever had," Wallace said.

"Well, you are wrong on this one," Dense said. "You are not going to work this case. You cannot investigate your own son's homicide. Go home, Wallace. And if Whick calls you again, he's off the case too."

Chapter 15

By Mark Kodama

Detective Wallace and Pedro sat at the vinyl-covered table in Wallace's mobile home. A CBS news anchor was reporting on the breaking Stormy Daniel scandal, "Adult film actress Stormy Daniel said 'Fear kept her from talking about an alleged affair with Donald Trump.' She told her complete story on 60 Minutes. It is already under attack by lawyer Michael Cohen, the president's personal attorney."

"You know I'd do anything to help you," Pedro told Wallace.

He shut off the TV and turned to Pedro.

"I know you would."

Pedro nodded. "I love you, man."

"Do you know something?" asked Wallace.

"I don't do what I used to do. Now I just clean pools..."

"And?"

"I could put you in touch with Three-Legged-Dan".

"Three-legged Dan?"

"He's a pimp. He runs a high-class escort agency called *Svetlana's Girls.*"

Wallace recognized the name from one of Johnny's cards.

"Is that so?"

"He always has his ear to the ground."

"Will he talk to me?"

"I will put in the word for you. *Todo por usted, Wallace.*"

"How do I find him?"

"Internet. Svetlana's Girls. Strictly high class. What happens in Vegas stays in Vegas. No pee tapes."

"Why do they call him Three-legged Dan?"

"Put it this way: when you see his silhouette, it looks like he has three legs. He is so big he would make John Holmes blush. He never wears short pants."

"I don't get it."

"You know, he's hung like a horse. If you were in the desert chased by the Manson family, you all could feel safe hiding behind his big one. They never would see you."

"I see…"

'*Verga.* I am worried."

"What?"

"You're slipping Wallace."

Chapter 16

By Kathryn Meyer

Wallace hadn't been to the Grand Aztec Hotel for years; not since he took his ex-wife to see Neil Diamond in the 80s. Cost him an arm and a leg; Johnny would have been five at the time.

Walking past the casino he pictured Johnny losing money by the thousands on the slot machines. Had he not put his career over his family, things may have worked out differently.

The old detective walked through the impressive glass doors of the Azure Bay and waited by the hostess stand. The air-conditioned restaurant was empty, except for a couple at the bar. The curious thing about Las Vegas casinos was that you could never tell whether it was day or night outside. It may as well have been midnight, as far as the couple was concerned. He was in a suit and she in a scanty cocktail dress; even if he could only see her from behind, it was clear she was a good 20 years younger than her companion. Wallace wanted to tell her: her future was in her own hands.

"Sorry to keep you waiting," said the hostess, striding over on her high heels. "Do you have a reservation?"

He hesitated. "Detective Wallace. I'm..."

"Oh, yes." She smiled. "Mr. Sánchez is expecting you. Follow me."

Both gave way to more than one busy waiter as they crossed out to the patio; this was where everybody was, feasting on large seafood platters and cold bottles of expensive white wine.

She indicated an empty table. Wallace noticed three wine glasses, chocolate crumbs on a dessert plate, and lipstick on two of the cloth napkins.

"He must be by the pool," said the hostess. "I'd look in the lounges."

There were lots of lounges in the pool area. Two more restaurants backed onto it and its sickening murmur of youth and amusement; waterfalls, palm trees. Bathers swam to a Tiki bar alongside the massive liver-shaped swimming pool, drinking exotic drinks while floating contently.

He recognized Three-Legged-Dan from a distance. Two striking women sat up on the nearby sun beds as Wallace approached.

"Like my office, Wallace?" Dan asked, rising from his couch by the pool.

"What's not to like?" Wallace replied, courteously lifting his hat at the ladies.

"Where's Pedrito? I was looking forward to seeing that *pinche-cabrón.*" He waved his hand at the women, prompting them to lie back down.

"He only cleans pools now," Wallace said.

Three-Legged Dan called a waiter's attention. He raised his Martini glass, gesturing invitingly at Wallace who respectfully declined the drink.

"Straight to business then. What can I do for you?

Wallace sat opposite him. He noticed the chain around his neck, the lighter in his see-through shirt pocket, the cut under his freshly shaved jaw and the two Kaftans hanging on the armchair beside him. As he rested his calf on his ankle, he noticed his espadrilles.

"I did a little investigating of my own..." said Three-Legged-Dan, leaning on the backrest. "...and we don't have your son on file. Our clientele is very exclusive."

Wallace pushed his shades up his nose.

"Look, I'm sorry for your loss and want to help. What are we looking for, exactly?"

Wallace patted his pocket, as though he was searching for notes, a photograph, something. Really, he was searching for the words.

He was totally unprepared. *Slipping*, as Pedro put it. Truth was he had nothing, nothing but Whick waving a photo of Johnny all around Vegas. And seeing as he hadn't heard from him, he probably didn't have anything either. He wished he still smoked.

"My son's murder was not only premeditated," he said finally. "It was executed by a skilled assassin. His blood alcohol concentration level was just 0.05. He wouldn't kiss a frog at the best of times, if you know what I mean."

"Well, when it comes to ass in Vegas, Three's your man. You can have our full catalogue of escorts; pretty, non-pixelated faces and all. Pedrito's very fond of you, you know. But I'll give you their names 'as and when' you get your leads. Three takes care of *all* his friends."

Three-Legged-Dan put his hand in his shirt pocket, pulling out a pen-drive. Not a lighter. *Slipping*. He was definitely slipping.

"Good old Pedro's vouched for you. It's all in here."

Wallace received it and put it in his pocket. He couldn't help but think that's just what he needed, a memory stick to store his past and shut it away in some drawer. He couldn't let this immeasurable sadness get in the way of finding John's killer. And he needed to do it soon.

"I gotta tell you though," said Three-Legged-Dan. "Svetlana's girls... they're under a strict non-disclosure agreement. You're gonna need a court order to get anything out of them."

"Of course."

"So, tell me, Detective. What does 'cleaning pools' stand for these days?"

Chapter 16

By Mark Kodama

There was no browner place on earth. The mountains were brown, the

hills were brown, and the plants and animals are brown. There was no

place more ugly or more beautiful than the desert. But it was a

dangerous place too. The bodies of a woman and her two young sons

were found after the woman stormed out of the car after a fight with her

husband. Walking in anger, Maria had become disorientated, turning

away from the highway rather than toward it. Her five-year-old boy

Peter was found in a dry creek bed. Maria's body was found five miles

away cradling her infant.

Wallace entered his mobile home. The thin aluminium door

slapped shut behind him. He went to his small refrigerator and grabbed

a beer. Looking at his protruding stomach he thought about his doctor

telling him he was pre-diabetic. He put the beer back and grabbed a

bottle of water. Lester Holt of NBC was interviewing the President.

"I was going to fire Comey, knowing there was no good time

to do it... In fact, when I decided to do it, I said to myself, 'You know

this Russia thing is a made-up story, an excuse by the Democrats for

having lost an election that they should have won...'"

Wallace opened his laptop computer and inserted the flash

drive he received from Three-legged Dan. He opened the only file

called "Danger." A series of beautiful naked women from all over world flashed on his computer screen. A video followed showing a female black widow devouring her mate.

The video ended with large flashing bold letters saying "Danger is Everywhere." Wallace called Lt. Dense who was not in. Wallace left a message and asked for a meeting.

Part II

Chapter 17

By Mark Kodama

Detective Bruce Wallace bounded up the steps and into the Las Vegas Metropolitan Police Department's headquarters. He flashed his badge as he passed by a long line of citizens waiting to pass through security. The uniform officer dressed in the tan dress shirt and slacks waived him through. A group of uniformed officers – black, white, Hispanic, Asians, men and women – gathered around Capt. Ross, a black man with closely cropped white hair. Times had changed since Wallace began as a rookie so many years ago, when the force was mostly made up of white men with female support staff. Capt. Ross smiled and nodded to Wallace as he passed by.

Wallace knocked on the office door of Lt. Dense. "Enter," responded the voice inside. Lt. Dense was standing behind his metal desk. The desktop was clear except for a pile of assorted files, photographs and papers piled in his in box. At the top of his file was Johnny's Rolex watch in an open evidence bag. A small circular trash can stood just to the left of his desk and beneath his in- box.

"Oh, Wallace. What brings you here? I thought you were taking some time off."

"I was."

"Sorry about your boy."

"Yeah," Wallace said pursing his lips tightly.

"Sit down."

The phone rang on Lt. Dense's desk.

"Speak," Dense said tersely. "Yes. No. I said Peabody was to handle that. Peabody! Okay." Dense hung up the phone and looked at Wallace.

"Speak."

"I met with somebody regarding Johnny's case – a confidential informant."

"I told you, you were off the case. Johnny is your son. You cannot investigate your own son's case."

"Yes . . . but."

"You are not on this case."

"I have some information you need to know."

"I said you are off the case. Dead, done, finito."

Wallace bit his tongue.

"I thought the Black Widows were wiped out years ago," he said quietly. "They may be back."

Dense began to breathe impatiently.

"Wallace you are a smart guy, but you have never learned to listen. That is why you were busted down to detective."

"Hear me out."

Dense looked at his watch. "Wallace, your time is up."

Wallace pulled his flash drive from his shirt pocket and handed it to Dense.

Dense tossed it on top of the pile of items in his inbox, next to Johnny's watch with the listening device planted by Davenport. The pile topped by Johnny's gold watch had grown so high it was beginning to teeter.

"This may save lives."

"I'll look at it," Dense said.

There eyes met. Wallace was skeptical.

"I'll call you," Dense said.

Chapter 18
By Garrison McKnight

Edna McFarland Wallace made a big entrance, as she always did. It was her son's funeral, nothing but the best for her boy. Jenny didn't want to be here today, but her boss agreed to pay her. Edna walked grim-faced down the aisle of the church, which was oversized for the number of people who would attend Big John's funeral. Several beautiful women all dressed in finery took up two rows in the church. Edna wondered how they knew her son. She was seated in the front, dabbing her eyes with a handkerchief.

Her ex-husband Bruce wandered in. You would think the man could have dressed up in a decent suit, not one he pulled out of a shoe! My God. She watched the man to whom she was once married, looking as if the light of life had abandoned him. Bruce Wallace walked slumped over and listless to the other side of the church. She pitied him.

A few of his detective friends sat around him, and of course, his beer buddy - that degenerate Pedro, the pool cleaner, was there too. Imagine Pedro with Bruce sitting right in front like he was immediate family. It disgusted Edna.

John Bruce Wallace lay in state at the front of the church. A beautiful hammered bronze coffin; nothing but the best for her boy. It had taken some time for the police to release his body. They wanted all the evidence they could get before they'd let her bury him. Her boy lay in the morgue for almost a week before they released him to her. The thought of it made her angry. They made him look good though. He looked as handsome in death as he had in life.

Edna eyed the congregants, most of them strangers. She wondered how they fit into Johnny's life, and then cried when she realized her little boy was dead. One thing she and Bruce always had in common was love for their son.

Edna was upset when she received his last credit card bill. If Johnny weren't dead, she would have killed him. He spent all his money on hookers, booze, and bars. If he was here now so she would cross examine him about a regular monthly payment he made to someone. She'd never noticed before, just paid his bills, but now with the murder, she was looking over his property, or her property rather, like a hawk. Someone was getting a sizable automatic withdrawal every month from Johnny's credit card. After the funeral, she was going to audit his finances with a fine-tooth comb.

The organ struck up a dirge, the music hanging heavy over the congregation. Edna cried again. Her loud, lamenting sobs reverberated throughout. People glanced at one another but tried to keep their faces forward, trying not to cry too. Tears streamed down the cheeks of more than one. Everyone knew Edna thought her son was lazy. Johnny never did an honest days' work and she had supported him for many years. Still, he had a beautiful home and a pool in the suburbs. No one questioned that Edna loved Johnny with all her heart.

As the minister stood to speak, a young woman with a little boy came and sat in the seat with all of the other ladies. Her name was

Carolina and she was known to be a dancer at The Frisky Pussy Cat, a
club Big John frequented. She sat stoically with a little blond boy,
about two-years-old, in her lap clinging to her neck.

The minister talked about how God had a big heart, room
enough for saints and sinners alike. He preached about deliverance,
forgiveness, murder, and the fact that Big John may not have lived the
life that most of us felt he should, but he was generous to a fault.

Yeah, with my money, thought Edna.

Bruce Wallace flinched as he listened to the minister. His
mind drifted, unwilling to accept what was being said. He was
annoyed detectives had not returned Johnny's gold watch back to him.
For all he knew it was still in Dense's office. What if somebody planted
a listening device in it? They would know everything about the
investigation.

Forensics did not find any prints. Dense had time to return the
watch. It had no evidentiary value to the investigation. He and Lt.
Dense never got along. The lieutenant would prefer that Wallace slink
out with his tail between his legs. He was jealous because Wallace had
solved some high-profile cases that the FBI wannabe couldn't. Dense
resented him for it.

The funeral ended, Edna and Wallace met eyes. There was
nothing left between them. *Now that their boy was gone, there was
definitely nothing, left between them.*

Carolina struggled to keep her little boy quiet. As Edna and
Wallace walked in front of Big John's coffin, the little boy ran into the
aisle in front of them, causing the procession to stop.

"Johnny!" Carolina hissed. Edna's head jerked up. The little boy looked strikingly like Johnny. That monthly payment on the credit card bill now made sense and filled Edna with unexpected hope on this darkest of days.

Chapter 19

By Bernice Groves

Ginger snap crumbs tumbled down the front of Erika's jogging suit.

Some bounced off her lap, falling onto the white tile floor; the rest found hiding places in the narrow folds of her garment. She frowned at them but didn't bother sweeping them away. She intended to eat two more anyway.

"More water?"

Erika looked at the waitress, a short brunette with curly hair and a wide smile. She held the pitcher with her left hand, her right hand holding it up from the base. A couple of fresh lemon slices floated around in the water. She glanced at her empty cup. She hadn't planned to get more, but it wouldn't hurt.

"Yeah, thanks."

A young man and his young daughter were eating breakfast together in the booth by the counter. He'd called her Bethany. The name rang several distant bells.

"Would you like anything else?"

Erika looked into the dark brown almost black eyes of the waitress and shook her head, attempting to smile, but the father's voice echoed in her mind. *Bethany.* Once upon a time, long ago in another life, she was Bethany.

And like a tide, it all came rushing back to her.

Bethany? That Bethany was dead.

"Never mind. I don't need anything. Thanks."

Erika walked back toward the doors to Jenny's Cafe. She slipped through the tinted glass doors, until the darkness of the doors made it impossible to distinguish between her and the crowd in the street.

Erika looked around. Only one other patron sat outside the café under an umbrella table. It was a shame too, with the good weather. From the looks of the sky, the good weather wouldn't last long either. She could even smell the slight hint of rain in the air, all earthy and damp, with the slightest hint of salt.

She'd never forget the smell of rain, and the distinct aroma it gave to freshly spilled blood, still warm from body heat. *Bethany*. Now that was a name she hadn't seen lately, especially not with these features. She shivered. She couldn't fight off the memory.

It was going on twenty odd years since the day rain mixed with blood and scattered her senses. She could still feel the stark contrast of her hot tears sliding down her cheeks and the icy kiss of raindrops against her warm skin.

"You can't die. I won't let you die," she'd moaned, resting her forehead against her father's. *"I called the cops. They'll be here any second."*

Her father's eyes, though, they just stared unendingly at the sky. It was such an intense stare, that she'd arched her neck to look up too. But there was nothing there, no approaching light, no god, only low-hanging, angry clouds. The emergency personnel carried her to the ambulance. She was bleeding from a gunshot wound to her right arm.

A few feet away, her father's lifeless body lay now face down in a pool of his own blood. He looked so strange lying there; too quiet, too stiff. She remembered that in a tiny part of her imagined he'd rise and kill her too, but he didn't. The shot she took had been true — the bullet sped right through his heart and into the distance. She thought she'd always remember the fear that crept into his eyes when he realized his life was done, but she hadn't.

It took her years to remember his face before the shot that killed him; before the nights he spent pacing the living room floor, peering out their windows and shooting at shadows. She hadn't known it then, only a child, but he was more than a simple CIA agent—he had enemies. He was an assassin. Sometime after an assignment gone wrong, the counseling sessions began, and then he stopped disappearing like he usually did and then, well, she watched her father slowly fade like a shadow before sunrise.

After the shot, child services came to take her away, but Aunt Lily wasn't having it. As her brother's sister, she had every right to step in to take care of her niece in light of such a tragedy, help get her the counseling she needed, help her forget the hands stained with her father's blood. Poor Aunt Lily. She meant well, but she didn't understand the scarring, the bloodstains. Her father would have understood.

Her dad was still a loving father except when he was having his flashbacks. He should've known she was a true shot, after all, he was the one that taught her.

Despite the dark memories floating around her mind, a faint smile lifted the corners of her lips; she hadn't seen Aunt Lily since she was sixteen. The years of monotony and pointless rules proved to be too much. Lily wanted her to attend church every Sunday and counseling sessions each week, where an old doctor stared at her through narrowed eyes like a spectator at a rare animal display. So, she disappeared. She ran away and didn't look back once, not even on the nights she found herself low on funds, chilled to the bone, rushing to complete an assignment for hot food in her stomach. The way she saw it, life was a series of choices. She had chosen her life, and her stomach was full.

Chapter 20

By Maria Jesu Estrada

Wallace sat at his kitchen barstool and imagined punching Lt. Dense

in the nose. Not only did Dense remove Wallace from the case, he

forced Wallace to take three week's bereavement leave. He nursed the

neat Buchanan's Special Reserve whiskey Johnny gave him as a

Father's Day's present, just last year, no doubt paid for with one of

Edna's credit cards. He kept the bottle in its blue shiny bag for months

in an abandoned cabinet. He breathed in the aroma. It was smooth, but

he preferred a simple Jack Daniels.

Pedro walked in and gave a long whistle. "So early jefe? It's like

8:00 a.m." Wallace marvelled at how this man, five foot nothing, had

once been one of the best assassins from the famed Estrada Colombian

cartel. Now he was a simple pool cleaner, but seventeen years ago, he

would have been riding around in a Rolls Royce, maybe a

Lamborghini, a woman in his front seat, and a flashy gun hidden from

view. Given the cartel rivalries, those joyrides only extended to the vast

hectares of the expansive *finca*. He now drove a black Honda Odyssey

for his wife and five kids, and the only things he was armed with were

the tools of his pool cleaning trade and that awful Bible he carried

everywhere.

Fifteen years ago Wallace had found him surrounded by five

neo-Nazis behind an old motel far away from the Vegas strip. Wallace had been called in for 401B near the sleazy motel, but when he got there all he found was a wino on the front sidewalk who had tripped and injured his knee.

To this day, Wallace still doesn't know why he walked behind the motel. Maybe it had been instinct, but there was Pedro in a tattered t-shirt and muddied jeans, shorter than his would be assailants, arms up in a fighting stance. The men were poised surrounding Pedro who was quite inebriated and barely able to stand.

Before he could stop the fight or say, "Las Vegas Police!" one of the men with a shiny bald head and stereotypical leather vest attacked. Wallace began to yell a warning, but Pedro gave such a forceful punch to the Nazi's face, that it knocked him out cold. The rest were going to jump him when Wallace pulled out his gun and shot into the ground. They took off running.

Wallace never broke the rules. He knew he should have called for backup and not discharged his weapon in a residential area, even if it was a cheap motel for hooking. Instead, Wallace gave Pedro forty dollars and told him to sober up and stay out of trouble.

"I owe you my life, Jefe," Pedro said at the time. He would later find out Pedro had a dark past. One he was running from.

Pedro's ties to the cartel were deep, but God interceded. A rival cartel eliminated almost all of the Estradas at a wedding, leaving Pedro to live his days in peace. Now, he was a Jehovah's Witness and married to the lovely Concha, a devout Christian.

Wallace had forgotten all about Pedro and was shocked, eight months later, when he showed up to clean their pool. Wallace insisted on paying him and only after great reluctance did Pedro accept.

Wallace convinced many at Metropolitan, including Capt. Ross, to hire him to clean their pools, too. Pedro soon hired a second person and then a third for his expanding pool cleaning business.

Wallace smiled at his friend, despite the terrible circumstances of Johnny's murder. Without being asked, Wallace poured Pedro two fingers.

"Did they return the watch?" asked Pedro.

"No, Dense said it was evidence." Wallace slapped his right leg. "This whole thing is wrong. There is something missing here, but I can't put my finger on it yet."

"I will keep looking, but Saturday, well you know. If I don't go worship, Concha will have my balls. So, I start again Sunday."

Wallace smiled despite the awful circumstances. "All this makes no sense, Pedro. Nothing came up on the database, and that idiot Dense temporarily revoked my password."

"Are they supposed to do that, boss?"

"Dense is trouble," Wallace said.

"¡Malparido!" said Pedro, lapsing into his old ways. He said a silent penitent prayer. "I wish I still drank, I could use one right now," Pedro bowed his head. "But I cannot break the vow I made to my wife."

Wallace's eyebrows perked up.

"I found out where the blonde might work..."

Chapter 21

L.T. Waterson

Erika stopped outside the club and tucked her hair up inside her hat.

Time to retrieve the knife.

No one looked up as she strode inside. It was almost lunchtime and the club was thinly populated. Most of the men were grouped close to the stage where a rather bored looking pole dancer was gyrating almost in time to the music. Erika didn't recognise her but then the club had a high turnover of staff and Erika seldom stripped during the day anyway.

At a table in the corner two men in suits were sitting, hunched together in conspiratorial fashion. Every so often they would steal glances towards the stage.

Erika did her best to discreetly scrutinize them. Perhaps they were two rival businessmen simply meeting in an out of the way location, but Erika committed their faces to memory anyway, just in case.

The knife was where she had left it and, relieved, she plunged her hand into the ice-cold water and drew it out. She tucked it away in her gym bag.

She flushed, hooked the bag over her shoulder and then proceeded to wash her hands.

On her way out of the club she passed the pole dancer. The girl smiled as the two passed but Erika did not smile back.

Now for phase two. Time to disappear.

#

Erika's long legs ate up the sidewalk as she headed back to her car. The sound of her sneakers scuffing against the asphalt had been joined by the tip tap, tip tap of a pair of heels.

Vegas was always busy. There was always someone tottering along in ridiculous heels no matter the time of day but Erika knew she was being followed.

Somebody was coming after her and Erika could feel her heartbeat pick up, feel the adrenaline flood her veins. Fight or flight and Erika nearly always picked fight.

She took a swift right and then a left and a short run took her to the entrance to the service alley running behind the clubs. Full of bins and rats and damp, very few people ever ventured there.

In the gloom and half-hidden behind a large bin Erika waited.

Tip tap, tip tap, the heels were getting closer. Then they rounded the end of the alleyway.

It was the pole dancer. The look on her face was no longer one of boredom but of murderous intent. Erika recognised that look.

The knife was in Erika's hand even before she remembered she had it. As the pole dancer reached to pull the piece of garrotting wire from her hair Erika clearly saw the black widow tattoo on her wrist.

Erika moved gracefully, her pose and poise almost balletic. Why would a Black Widow be coming after her?

The pole dancer shrugged and Erika frowned. Better finish this now.

She spun, moving just that little bit faster, hoping to catch her assailant off guard.

The other girl moved with her.

Now!

Erika dashed forward. Moving dangerously close, she swung the knife into her opponent's left leg, then stepped back as she fell to the ground writhing in pain.

Eyes cold, Erika stood over the helpless girl. "Who sent you? If you do not tell me, I will finish you off. "

"D...Davenport," the word was hissed from a mouth twisted with pain.

That figured. Time to go. Erika shoved the knife back into her bag and ran.

Chapter 22

By **Mark Kodama**

Erika hated to be in this position but she needed help from The Ghost,

now calling himself Roman Santini. Erika could possibly disappear with Chiara but then again they would never really feel safe. Davenport eventually would find them. If anybody could take down Davenport, it would be The Ghost.

She thought about the last time she saw Chiara. "This is your big sister," Ya Ya said. Little Chiara bounded forward and squeezed her tight. She was an angel. Big round face with a wide smile. She was pure and innocent, unsullied by the world and the compromises one must make to get by.

Tears rolled down Erika's face and they embraced. And Erika never cried. Not even at her father's funeral. Erika thought of her father.

Her father looked so peaceful as he lay in his suit in his open coffin. She could see his smile, feel the warmth of his breath and hear his laughter. But he looked . . . so inanimate – like a mannequin. Was he ever alive? Others cried, but not Erika.

"We are gathered here today . . ." she could hear the minister say.

It all seemed like a dream – even while it was happening. "Poor child," one old woman said and patted her head. It was all she could do not to jump up and rip her head off.

Aunt Lily, eyes full of tears, tried to hug her but Erika pushed her away and glared at her. Lily took a step back and stopped crying. "Strange child," she said almost to herself.

Erika thought of her father. She loved him so.

Chapter 23

By Silvana McGuire

Find a new beginning, a new start in life. Roman Santini was waiting in the back of the limousine in the front entrance of his headquarters building. The driver opened the door and she slid into the back of the black sedan without missing a step. Santini - The Ghost, Hudson - was dressed in a white tux with a black tie. Erika looked like a movie star with dangling jewelry, classic make up and red designer dress. The chauffeur, a beautiful young woman dressed in black uniform and cap, smiled. Her smile was friendly but her eyes malevolent.

"Where are we going?" Erika was expecting a business-like evening but this seemed a bit more elaborate.

"You will see," was his reply as he entwined his arm on hers and helped her sip from his own champagne glass. Always a gentleman, he had a romantic streak tonight that amused her. She was used to being all things to all people. If he wanted a high fashion model today, and the price was him helping her earn her freedom from Davenport, then that's what he was going to get.

"Now you must know, I am not easily surprised…" she ran a fingernail over his face and under his chin. His cologne was a bit strong but the champagne was first class. Another smell hit her senses; his cologne, it was the same one her father used to wear.

He hugged her and easily laid his body on top of hers on the limousine seat. Suddenly, her Black Widow trained senses picked up another assassin in the neighborhood.

His breath was hot, and her mouth found its way to his. Drinking from each other, the forgotten champagne spilled on the floor of the limousine. Erika was used to handling customers seeking her many skills, but something was off. Her head was spinning, her heart was pounding and his touch made her shudder. At that moment she recognized the strange smell in the air.

Cyanide.

She understood and knew what to do. She pushed him away and jumped towards the privacy window splitting the driver from the back of the car. She used the heel of her shoe to break the glass. The driver was wearing a state-of-the-art filter on top of her mouth and nostril. The Black Widow was poisoning them via the air-conditioning!

Horrified, even more than a bit drowsy, Roman retreated to one side of the seat and watched as Erika took off her fashionable right earring and held the long stem in her closed fist. She stabbed the Black Widow in the jugular. The limo veered out of traffic and crashed into a vacant building along the street as blood from the driver spurted all over the front seat.

Santini felt sick as the champagne came back into his throat and he puked on his white tuxedo. Perplexed, he realized he was puking blood and called Erika for help.

A man who was filling his gas tank before heading out of town later provided this account of the events that unfolded next:

"I noticed the limo first. It was all shiny and black and beautiful, but it was going way too fast for this road. I yelled at Susan to watch out because she had her headphones on for that damn phone of hers. We both saw the limo fly by so fast it looked like the tires weren't even touching the road. I still don't understand how that's even possible! That's when it turned into that dirt patch over there…"

He gasped for air. He was speaking so fast that he had forgotten to breathe. His companion, Susan, took over the narrative for the eager citizen reporter filming them on her small camera phone.

"All right, all right, Jack. You'll be all right." She patted him on the back to try and calm him down. "We saw a lot of dirt and smoke coming out of that patch of weeds they drove into and then they turned around and came back straight towards us! They were out of control so we ran our butts off and hid in there." She pointed to the gas station convenience store. Onlookers and a police car were surrounding the spot, all captured by the small camera of the citizen journalist.

The limo had crashed into a nearby store front. Erika limped away from the wreckage, barefoot with her high heels in hand. She was on the run.

Chapter 24
By P.C. Darkcliff

Erika left the dressing room and scanned The Man Cave Strip Club in

Martinsburg, West Virginia. She needed a place to hide until she could

decide what to do. The tables were full; the clientele pathetic. Some

patrons drooled into their beer while ogling the dancers. Others glanced

around like prairie dogs, waiting for a chance to grab a passing stripper

by the ass. As they looked too cheap to spend a twenty on a lap dance,

she headed for the bar counter.

A stout, hoary man sat on the farthest stool, a cocktail in his

hand. He sported a black tailor-made suit and more gold than an Aztec

king.

She walked up to him, swaying her hips and sticking out her

breasts. "Hi there, handsome," she said, placing her manicured hand on

his shoulder. "Would you like a lap dance?"

He grinned and licked his lips, "Why not?"

She glanced at his rings shining on his fingers and said, "Fifty

bucks."

He glanced at her nipples poking at her black mini dress and

said, "Fine."

She smiled and led him to the back of the joint. He put his arm

around her back and instinct told her she was in danger. She shifted her

eyes toward the hand that rested on her shoulder and gasped. One of his rings had a diamond that was half as big as a ping pong ball. Suddenly, she realized she'd seen that ring before; it was a weapon Davenport assigned for especially important hits.

Davenport had once loaned her the ring to kill a Bulgarian mafia boss. She'd picked up the Mafioso in the bar of his hotel. As they later entered his room, she'd pressed the diamond against his neck and pressed the side of the ring to release a tiny poisoned dart. The Mafioso had groaned, gone rigid like a board, and tumbled to the floor. He'd died in spasms. And now Davenport had sent this guy to use the same weapon on her.

Davenport must have guessed she would be wary of women but would drop her guard around men. And he'd guessed right.

"I'm Nick," the man said, squeezing her shoulder.

Erika gulped and nodded. She wanted to wriggle out of his embrace and run. The deadly diamond was three inches from her ear, though. A wrong move and he would poison her.

A bald security guard called Greg stood in the hallway that led to the lap dance booths. As they passed him, she tried to make eye contact. However, it wasn't her *eyes* that had Greg's attention.

Her heart leaped against her ribcage as they entered the first booth. Nick grabbed her hips and pulled her toward him. He could kill her with a twist of his hand.

He whispered in her ear, "Do you know who I am?" His breath felt hot and sticky on her earlobe, like a steaming sponge.

She said nothing.

"I'm a naughty boy. Oh yes, a naughty, naughty boy. Spank me!"

Erika breathed in relief. So he played a perv to distract her. That gave her a few more minutes to live and think.

He hardened against her stomach. That bastard wanted fun before he murdered her. Well, she would let him have it.

"Oh, you naughty boy," she whispered into his ear.

Then she stepped back and rammed her knee into his balls. As she closed her hand into a fist to crush his larynx, she noticed he moaned in pain, grabbed his crotch, and gawked at her in disbelief.

No hit-man would do that. At least not a hit-man Davenport would send after her.

Erika grabbed his hand and inspected the diamond ring. She saw no button or trigger; it was a harmless jewel adorning a harmless pervert. And she was a paranoid bitch.

"I'm sorry, Nick."

"What the hell, bimbo?" Nick groaned, tears streaming out of his eyes. "I said I wanted my ass spanked, not my balls crushed. You always go the extra mile, bitch?"

She was about to apologize again when she heard footsteps. She turned around and saw Greg stomping toward them.

Erika guessed that Nick would complain and the boss would fire her. She wasn't sorry about losing that job. All she felt was relief that Davenport had backed off. Nobody had tried to murder her in a while. That was a good sign.

Then she noticed that Greg held a gun with a silencer. He walked to the moaning Nick and with no hesitation sent a bullet through the man's forehead.

Nick staggered and collapsed. Blood and brains gushed out of the hole in his head and pooled on the floor.

Erika staggered as well. "Why the hell did you do that?"

"Because he was about to make a fuss," Greg said, "and the boss would come and kick you out."

"So?"

Greg smirked. "If the boss kicked you out, I would lose a chance to do this." He pointed the gun at her head.

Erika gasped. "So Davenport really sent a guy this time, huh?"

Greg nodded and grinned. "And he pays damned well."

She glanced into the hallway. Nobody had heard the shot. Nobody was coming to help. Deceit was the only thing that could save her.

She looked at Nick's corpse and recoiled as if she'd seen him move. Greg frowned and followed her gaze.

Erika ducked under the gun's line of fire, lifted her hands, and grabbed the side of the silencer to turn the gun against him. Greg groaned when she kicked his knee and jammed the gun into his belly. She yanked the gun out of his hand and fired. The bullet bored through his neck. He gurgled and fell on top of Nick.

As Greg wheezed toward death, Erika wiped the gun on Nick's tie, kicked it into a corner, and slipped out of the booth. Walking across the joint toward the exit, she realized that Davenport wouldn't give up. She had to do something.

Chapter 25
By Nerisha Kemraj

Reaching his mother's home in Parker, doing a routine check up,

Wallace replaced the damaged mailbox. Unable to take care of herself any longer, his mother now lived at a nursing home in Las Vegas.

A surge of memories flashed through his mind. It felt good to be back in his childhood home. This place held memories of Johnny, too. His son spent most of his time with his grandmother as he and Edna focused on their jobs, which took up most of their time, unlike the usual nine to five jobs. So Wallace's mother practically raised Johnny. Worn out from the long day, Wallace chose to spend the night.

He awoke to screaming from the house next door. His head hurt. Disoriented, he realized he'd fallen asleep on the sofa. He staggered to the kitchen and filled the kettle.

It was 3 a.m. He needed coffee, and he would not be able to catch any more winks with the ruckus going on next door.

He switched the TV on, holding his steaming cup of coffee. The aroma alone shook him awake.

The politics on television added to his headache. Donald Trump again. *Never has anyone else dominated American news as much as President Trump has,* Wallace thought. Switching the TV off, he threw the remote across the room.

The doorbell rang.

Who could that be?

Never mind. They must know he was asleep and hopefully go away. He was not in the mood for any drama.

It rang again.

"Please help me. Open up." The voice of a woman carried through the door.

Looking through the peephole, Wallace noticed a young woman, in her early twenties. He winced at the gold piercings embellishing her face: above her right eyebrow, through her nose and above her lips. Her hairstyle boasted a closely cropped left side, while her hair remained long on the right side.

"What is it?' he said, with the door still closed. He'd been in the game too long to trust a situation at face value.

"I'm at the house next door. My boyfriend and I were arguing. You must've heard us. He's violent. I had to get out of there. I need to make a call. Please."

He'd seen enough violence toward women. "All right," he felt sorry for her and opened the door. She stepped inside and he closed it behind her. "The telephone's there," he indicated with a nod of his head, noting that she didn't seem as shaken up as one would have expected.

"Thank you," she said, turning to the phone. "And can I please have a glass of water?"

Hearing him pour the water for her, Heidi pretended to be on a call.

Wallace glimpsed a small spider tattoo on her back as she turned and his muscles tensed. He grabbed his Glock without her noticing. This would not end well.

"Here's your water," he said, turning, with his gun trained towards her. But she was already waiting with a silencer at the end of her pistol.

"Put it down old man," she said.

"You first."

She laughed. "You aren't gonna make this easy are you?"

"What do you want?"

"The same thing I always want. Money. And you're in my way of getting it."

"Did someone send you?" he asked.

Her jaw tightened.

Following him from the funeral in her disguise was the easy part, but waiting around for the opportune time to strike had been tasking. And Davenport wanted him to die a slow and painful death.

Her lips curled into a smile. She lived for pain.

"Turn yourself in and this doesn't have to get messy," he said.

"Messy for you? Or messy for me? Let me tell you, I'm a fan of messy, myself. Besides, the cleanup is refreshing," she laughed, her head tilting backwards.

This was all the time Wallace needed. In an instant he grabbed a hold of her gun but she held it steady. As small built as she was, she proved to be stronger than expected. Using him as anchorage she swung her feet, kicking both of his out from under him. His body hit the floor with a loud thud. Both their weapons flew into the air, landing a few feet away from them. They wrestled on the ground. Heidi dug into Wallace's arms with her nails which were sharpened to mini daggers. She slammed her customized bracelet down onto his nose and he swore loudly, endured the pain through gritted teeth.

Heidi reached for the gun concealed in her stockings but Wallace grabbed her and flung her across the room.

He grabbed his Glock. An injured Heidi fired a shot in his direction but missed. Wallace returned fire. His second shot hit her in her chest.

Chapter 26
By Chris Irons

It felt good to be out of West Virginia. Perhaps it was the inspiration of the soaring skyscrapers letting her know anything was possible or maybe it was the sweat of survival from everyone in the city that hung in the air. It had been some time since she had been to New York **City, with** its dreams and survival of the fittest attitude which fueled Erika. She smiled as her stilettos clicked along the crowded sidewalks. She had taken the red-eye flight from Las Vegas and would red-eye it back there.

The power of overcoming any obstacle filled her this morning. After many sleepless nights worrying about finances, she had a clear answer. After double-crossing Davenport there would be no going back to **his** money and stripping was only a young woman's income. Deciding to work with Wallace meant prison, which was unacceptable. She dreamed of living in a seaside home perhaps in a small obscure village in Italy with little Chiara. That plan took money.

Erika entered the twenty-eight-story building in downtown Manhattan and took the elevator to the Law Offices of Armstrong and White. One of R. Colton Armstrong, Jr.'s premier clients was James Davenport. Mr. Armstrong was expecting a Dorothy Parker.

Erika flipped her wig's raven hair over her shoulder and checked the manila folder in her Gucci brief case as the elevator doors opened.

"Ms. Parker?" the receptionist inquired.

"Yes," Erika lied, turning her face away from the security camera.

"Mr. Armstrong asked me to bring **you** right in. Follow me."

The receptionist led Erika to the corner office. R. Colton Armstrong, Jr., looked up. His eyes narrowed and his jaw ever so perceptibly tightened. He stood up and came around from his large walnut wood desk. He had a perfectly clipped silver hair with a tanned face from his recent Florida vacation with his wife and teen-aged children home for spring break from their expensive prep school.

"Hello, Mr. Armstrong. Nice office," Erika said, looking around.

Armstrong's face tightened.

"Can we speak confidentially?" Erika asked.

"Of course, ah, Ms. Parker**, was it?** Please have a seat," Armstrong turned to the receptionist "Sherry, hold all my calls, will you please?"

"Yes, Mr. Armstrong," she said, closing the door with a soft click on her way out.

"This manila folder contains pictures of you, and me, and my whip from your last business trip to Vegas. Look how much fun **we're** having."

Erika slid the file across the walnut desk to him.

He quickly flipped through the photos. "Well, you must be mistaken. These are not me," he smiled cheerfully. "Are these your only copies?"

Erika smiled.

"What can I do for you?" he asked.

"Suppose I need to get a message to our mutual acquaintance, James. Could I contact you?" She flashed a photo of her and James Davenport. She smiled at Armstrong's recognition of their mutual friend.

"I don't know how I can help you in this regard."

"My friend, Dorothy Parker, will leave you a message."

"How can I contact you?"

"There will be no need. I'll contact you."

Erika glanced at her watch. "Oh, I'm late for my next appointment. I'll be in touch."

Part III

Chapter 27

By Garrison McKnight

Wallace fumed when he returned to his trailer. Dense had forced him to take three weeks leave but he'd be damned if he'd walk away from Johnny's murder. Dense had to be pretty stupid to think he would. With Dense in charge of the investigation, things were going nowhere. There would be more deaths, and Johnny's murderer never would be brought to justice.

The old detective sat on the couch. *Ah to hell with it. I need a beer.* He drank a beer. And another. The television was boring. Neither the beer nor the boob tube took away the anger in his heart. He couldn't give up on the investigation. He would do it without the help of the Las Vegas Metropolitan Police Department.

Most of his friends at Metropolitan were great. But that Dense...Exhausted, Wallace decided to turn in for the night. Funny how tired he was until he crawled into bed. He couldn't shut his brain off. The mess he made of his life with Edna...He also should have given Johnny the attention he deserved. No wonder his son was so screwed up. Now look how things turned out.

He heard a car drive past his trailer. That was curious. There wasn't too much traffic out this way. He listened until he could no longer hear it before finally drifting off to sleep.

Erika picked the lock on the old trailer. It was so cheap she was quickly inside before quietly closing the door behind her. She saw the few bottles of beer on the table, and Wallace's gun lying there too. She shook her head thinking the cop was slipping. She would use Wallace's gun against him. As she silently moved toward his covered body, she heard the cocking of a pistol.

"Where do you think you're going?" Wallace asked, pointing his gun. Erika handed him the pistol. Wallace motioned her to sit down. He turned on the light.

"Wallace, I need your help," she said.

Wallace stared at her.   "Who are you?" Erika could feel the knife in her boot but she was not here to harm Wallace.

"We have a mutual enemy."

"What do you mean?" Wallace said. He held the pistol at her, noticing for the first time her black widow tattoo on her right arm.

"A man named Davenport wants to kill you, and then he wants to kill me. Maybe we can help each other by working together."

"Davenport?" Wallace was confused.

"Yes, you killed his mother many years ago."

"Stella." The light went on in Wallace's head.

"The original black widow."

Wallace thought of Stella. The look of defiance in her face before he shot her dead. In a flash, Erika snatched the gun from his hand and trained it on him.

"I'm sorry Wallace," she said, her eyes narrowed ever slightly as she levelled the gun at him. "I have not come to kill you, but to propose a deal to you."

"You killed my son," Wallace said through his clenched teeth. He wanted to kill her right then.

"Davenport ordered the hit and now he wants to kill you," Erika said.

"What are you proposing?" Wallace asked.

"We join forces against Davenport. I can lead you to him. For now, though, I'll give you time to think about my offer. I'm leaving. I will leave your gun outside. Do not leave here until I am gone and then wait five minutes or I will come back and kill you.

"How can I contact with you?"

"I will contact you in a few days to give you time to make a decision."

She walked swiftly and silently backwards out of the trailer, covering her tracks, leaving in her car.

Chapter 28
By Angelika Delf

"The situation cannot go on like this, Mr. Wallace."

Wallace nodded. The next day he had rushed to the Desert Rose Nursing Centre, after he had received a call from the staff.

"It's been three days now. Madame Giselle refuses to eat. She will not listen to anyone and speaks only French."

That was his mother alright. Anytime she would get upset, she would completely ignore everyone around her.

"I'm afraid we will have to put her on medical assistance. We are responsible for her care."

"Let me talk to her, Ms. Jones."

Wallace walked down the long hallway like he had done nearly every weekend for the last two years, passing the nursing station and the dozen residents in the long corridor lined with mostly old men and women sitting in their wheel chairs in various stages of decay, all nearly at their life's end. A dark-haired young man in his twenties sat in his wheelchair staring vacantly into space as two old residents sat in their wheel chairs talking excitedly to each other, gesticulating with their hands to illustrate a point. The ever present and strong smell of disinfectant and the faint smell urine and feces hung in the air like the faint smell of decay on a hot summer's evening. But no one seemed to notice.

He oftentimes tried to get Johnny to come with him but he always had an excuse. It was not that Johnny did not love his grandmother but that he had loved his grandmother too much. Wallace felt guilty that he had not spent enough time with his son growing up: his first steps, his first day at school and the baseball games. There were always new criminals to catch and new cases to solve. Wallace felt the weight of protecting the public against the evil of the world. But he felt guilty that his son had paid the price of his and Edna's busy work schedules.

Johnny had been mostly raised by Wallace's mother, the living and overindulgent matriarch of the family. Wallace's own father had died when he was but a boy and his mother had single-mindedly devoted her own life solely to him, never remarrying.

When he reached his mother's room, a Nigerian nurse dressed in green scrubs grabbed her clipboard and casually walked by heading for the room next to his mother's where Ms. Betty screamed, "They are coming to get me!"

He took a deep breath and reached in his pocket for a mint candy to cover his bad breath. He tapped on the door. No answer. His mother was probably sleeping.

Two weeks ago, when he told her that her Johnny died, he thought that he would lose her too. She fainted. When she awoke, they both wept bitter tears. When he came to see her again, she greeted him with a big smile and an old photo of herself and Wallace and Johnny.

She asked him how Johnny was. She said she missed him and he should bring him sometime to visit her.

He closed his eyes, put on his happy face and entered the room. He took a quick look around. The adjustable hospital bed was empty. Jesus on the cross hung on a leather necklace from the corner of the board above her bed. Johnny's picture frame was lying on the night stand next to the bed.

Giselle sat in her velvet French armchair, next to the window. She had her socks on, sitting straight, her right hand clenching her wooden carved walking stick, staring at the dark of the night.

"Hello, mom," Wallace said. "Bonsoir, maman."

"Bonsoir, mon chéri." She kept on staring outside. "Comment tu vas, mon cœur?"

"Better, now that I see you."

Her eyes fluttered, she turned her head and smiled at him as she always did, the same warm loving smile he had always known. "I have missed you, chéri." She stretched out her arms and kissed him on his forehead.

"I heard you gave the nurses a hard time, mom," he smiled at his mother and sat at the corner of the bed.

"No. Just taking care of business," she smiled back. Her face darkened.

"How is Johnny?" she asked.

Wallace turned gray. 'He is fine, mom," he managed to swallow.

Gielle looked right in his eyes.

"What is troubling you, Wallace?"

"Oh, nothing mom."

"I know something is troubling you. Please tell me."

"Well, I have this friend . . ."

"You are always thinking of others Wallace."

He could feel his voice start to falter and his eyes began to
tear.

"Take your time, son. I am here."

"I have this friend, you know, another detective."

"*Oui.*"

"A woman, a professional assassin, lured his son into a trap
and killed him."

"Oh la la, c'est terrible."

"My detective friend swore on his son's grave to find this
killer and bring her to justice."

"*Oui.*"

"Well, he found her. And she admitted to my friend that she
had killed her son."

"Your poor friend."

"Turns out she was hired by an old enemy of his, a Mr. X.
My detective friend killed Mr. X's mother trying to arrest her."

"Hate only begets more hate."

"Now this lady assassin who killed my friend's son is offering
to lead him to her boss. She said he is trying to kill her."

" Je n'aime pas ça. I surely don't like this. Maybe a trap."

"She is the only way he can get to him."

"Did he notify his superiors?"

"Useless."

"Hmmm."

"Should he take a chance and work with this killer? It is the only way he can get to Mr. X."

His mother thought for a moment.

"The only way?"

"Yes, mother."

"Nothing in life is certain. But if you only have bad options, you must choose the best one."

"I see."

Her eyes hardened. "Wallace, work with her if you must. But do not turn your back on her. And kill her if you can." His mother sighed, "The old days were much simpler. Sure, they were not fair. But something also has been lost."

Chapter 29

By Garrison McKnight

Edna McFarland Wallace was not going to be deterred. She decided to find out who Carolina Andrews was. She wanted to confirm who was the father of Carolina's son. Edna allowed the automatic withdrawal on the credit card to continue after Johnny's death.

Manny Fleming was the best P.I in Vegas. She would be patient and let Manny do his job. Jenny's voice came through on the speaker on her office phone. "Mr. Fleming is here for his appointment."

"Send him in," Edna said.

Manny Fleming may have been the best in the business, but he had a slimy air about him. He was dressed in a frumpy suit holding an envelope in his hand. Edna stood and offered him a seat. Edna often used Manny to try to catch people making false claims against the insurance companies. It wasn't uncommon for Manny to find them roofing, playing basketball or working out at the gym when they claiming total disability.

"It's all here." Manny slid the manila envelope across her desk. Edna looked him in the eye.

"Well?" she asked, impatiently.

"It appears your son had a child with Carolina Andrews."

Edna's eyes widened. Why hadn't Johnny told her he had a son? She pulled out the contents of the envelope. A birth certificate naming John Bruce Wallace as the father, and picture of little Johnny with John in the swimming pool.

The private investigator had taken the pictures from Carolina's phone. It hadn't been easy without her knowledge. He'd even gotten a hair sample from the little boy's jacket at the playground. Running a DNA test against her Johnny proved without a doubt, little Johnny was Edna's grandson.

Edna wrote out a check right then and there. Thanking Manny for a job well done, she asked him to see himself out.

Edna called Bruce on the phone, just as Manny closed the door. She left him a message. His cell phone was a piece of crap, and like his car, it never worked. He couldn't be reached at the office now that he was on leave.

She decided Carolina could live in Johnny's house to raise her grandson. The house now, again, belonged to her since she had also been on the title. Johnny had a life estate and the ownership of the property reverted to Edna upon his death.

When Edna saw Little Johnny, her heart softened. She and Bruce loved their son. She knew this was the one thing they had in common. She knew that Wallace was hurting as much as she was. Maybe Bruce could get a second chance in raising his grandson and wouldn't screw things up so bad this time, now that he was older and wiser. Nothing would be too good for her grandson.

***

Lt. Dense sat in the chair of his office. Det. Peabody handed him another file to review. Dense put it in his in box, inadvertently knocking Johnny's Rolex watch into the small steel circular trash can next to his desk.

***

Davenport sat in his office, staring his computer with his head set on. He was listening to Dense's conversations through the listening device he had implanted in Johnny's watch. He heard the crash of the watch clanging against metal and then silence.

Chapter 30
By Jim Bates

Wallace spun the combination dial of his gun safe, taking comfort in the clicking of the tumblers. The visit from Erika had focused his mind like a mountain lion on its prey. Davenport had to die. Erika, too, of course, but first Davenport. He reverently removed his guns: two Glocks, and set them on the kitchen table. Then he began cleaning them, obsessively, over and over and over. But as the minutes went by and turned to hours, his anger grew exponentially until he was on-fire, burning with nearly uncontrollable rage. He was bent on revenge and he was going to have it. Davenport was going down.

Finally, when the guns were gleaming and spotless, smelling of gun oil and man sweat, he set them aside, poured a shot glass of whiskey and tried to calm down. He couldn't get his mind off his son. God, he may not have been the perfect father, but they'd had a pretty good life together, especially the early years.

Damn it! He smacked his hand hard on the table causing the whiskey glass to nearly tip over. Johnny was gone. Gone forever. He was so pissed off that when his cell rang for the tenth time in ten minutes, he nearly threw the damn thing out the door into the desert. Damned Edna. To hell with it and anyone else who had the nerve to call him. He just wanted to be left alone.

But after more unrelenting ringing, he picked up the phone and glanced at the display. *Pedro.* Maybe he has information on where this girl works.

"What's going on!" he answered. "Any news?"

"Hola, boss," Pedro said. Wallace could see him grinning on the other end. Funny guy.

"Look, I've got a lot going on,"

"I know and I want to help."

"Any news on where this girl works?"

"Not yet."

"What's up, then?"

"I think we should team up."

"Thanks, Pedro but this is something I am going to do myself."

Pedro laughed. "Jefe, do you hear yourself? You sound like a deranged cowboy. This isn't some gunfight at a corral in Dodge City. This is the real deal. Davenport and his men have enough guns for a small army. You're going to need help. You may be walking into a trap. You going to need me if you are to avenge your son."

"No, I've told you before, I'm doing this my own. My way."

"Listen, Frank Sinatra. Or can I just call you Frank? Your way is ridiculous. You can't go after a psychopath like Davenport all alone. He won't play fair, doesn't know the meaning of the word. And you can't trust that broad either."

One thing about Pedro, Wallace thought to himself, if nothing else he could wear you down. It wouldn't hurt to listen. "Okay, what do you want then?"

"You at the trailer?"

"Yeah." Outside the wind was picking up, driving grains of sand into the cheap aluminum siding, pounding it like buckshot. "Why?"

"I'll be right over. We can work out a plan."

"I told you, no!" he yelled. "What don't you understand?"

"Here's what you don't understand, my friend. I love you, man. I owe my life to you. If it wasn't for you who knows where I'd be now. God works in mysterious ways, jefe."

"Look..."

"Look nothing. If it wasn't for you, I'd never have met my beautiful Concha. She's the love of my life. I owe that to you."

"And you'd risk that for me?"

"Yes. Besides, nothing's going to happen to us, right? We're the good guys."

"Okay, fine," he gave in, sighing. "I'll be waiting." He paused for a moment, listening to the wind whistling across the desert, rattling the windows. He was lucky to have a friend like Pedro. "I guess I should thank you."

"Hey. Johnny was your boy. You want justice. So do I."

An hour later there was a knock on the door and without a word Pedro stepped inside. Wallace came out from the back to greet him. The two men looked at each other. Pedro was amazed at the transformation. Gone was the disheveled person he'd last seen. Instead, the man before him stood straight and tall and was bright eyed and smoothly shaven. He wore pressed tan slacks, a clean, white, snap button shirt and a bolo tie centered with a turquoise stone. On his feet were polished hand tooled cowboy boots and on a nearby table was what looked like a brand new Panama hat. In that moment Pedro knew Wallace was back.

Wallace took a step forward and clasped hands with Pedro. He could see it in his friend's clear blue eyes. This man was going to take no prisoners.

"I'm glad you're here." Wallace said grimly.

"Me, too," Pedro answered, suddenly feeling Wallace's power. He smiled, "Let's sit down and figure out how we're going to kill that son-of-bitch Davenport."

Wallace led the way to the table where he carefully set aside the Glocks. Then the two men sat down, and began laying out their plan.

Chapter 31

By Mark Kodama

Wallace watched a group of teen-agers playing basketball on the asphalt court. He could hear music from an ice cream truck in the parking lot and the distant shouts of a baseball game. A young woman with sunglasses, dressed like a teen-ager in a jogging suit walking a small dog, approached. She sat down on the wood bench next to him.

He set his newspaper in his lap and nodded to the young woman. She let her sunglasses slip down her nose. Peering over the lenses, she asked, "Wallace?"

"Erika," he said, thinking, *She's good – real good.*

"Made up your mind yet."

"Not yet."

"I can bring you to Davenport."

"How?"

"He wants me to deliver you to him so he can kill you himself."

"Why don't you do that?"

"Because he will kill me afterward."

"Why?"

"It's a long story."

"How can I trust you? You killed my son."

"How can I trust you?"

"You can't."

"Exactly. We are not asking for trust."

"Why are we talking then?"

"We both have no choice."

"After we kill Davenport, what next?"

"We both will do what we have to do."

"I see."

"I hear Lt. Dense is in charge of things."

"How do you know this?

"The walls have ears."

"He's a good man."

Erika laughed, "Then why does he ignore what you have to say?"

Wallace was quiet.

"There is a listening device in Johnny's watch and its sitting on Lt. Dense's desk. Like I said, we both have no choice."

"What next?"

"I left instructions for you in an envelope in your trailer."

Chapter 32

By Mark Kodama

Pedro pulled up in his wife's Black Toyota Odyssey, it was more reliable than the old Plymouth. Wallace waited outside his trailer and glanced at his watch. Fifteen minutes early. Although it was eight a.m., it was already hot.

Wallace checked his weapons: two 9 mm Glocks and a knife. He hoped that he could finish off Davenport in a final showdown. He would deal with Erika later.

"*Jefe*, "Pedro said and smiled.

"Pedro," Wallace replied. "I don't really know how to thank you."

"You already have."

When they arrived at Union Station, they went to the fast food court to await further instructions.

An old man dressed in a blue uniform was sweeping the tile floor. An old woman hunched slightly forward approached them from behind.

"Wallace," said the old woman in a young woman's voice, "it's me, Erika. Don't turn."

"Alright," Wallace acquiesced.

"Are you Pedro?" Erika asked.

"Yes, ma'am," Pedro said.

"I hear you're good with a gun."

Pedro shrugged his shoulders. "Pool cleaning brush too."

"Garage. Land Rover. Wallace, you drive," said Erika.

"You better let me drive," Pedro said.

"Okay, you drive," agreed Erika. "Walk in front of me." The two men took the lead.

"Check it out. I still have a nice ass after all these years," Pedro proudly announced.

They drove down Fremont streets past the Bellagio Fountain and the great casinos of the strip: MGM, Caesar's Palace and the Mirage. As decided, Pedro drove. Wallace sat next to him the front passenger seat and Erika sat in the back seat behind Pedro. She removed her wig and disguise.

Pedro headed out on Interstate 15 toward California. Driving the opposite way into Las Vegas at night still gave Wallace chills, the way the lights shot up into the sky like some giant alien space craft landing in the middle of desert.

"*Jefe, d*on't look back, but we are being followed," Pedro remarked.

Wallace looked into his passenger side rear view without turning his head. Erika pulled her compact mirror from her purse, pretended to add a dusting of makeup while looking behind them. A white Chevrolet.

"I'm speeding up," Pedro said. "I think that black SUV behind the white Chevrolet is following us too."

"The black mirrored sunglasses give them away," Wallace said.

"Erika, do you see them?"

"Got it," she said and put her Berretta in her lap, right hand on the trigger. It would be difficult for Davenport's men to see her through the smoked windows. Pedro and Wallace drew their guns. Pedro opened his window, the hot desert air blasted his face and roared in his ears.

Pedro moved to the slower lane on the far right. The white Chevrolet followed him.

The SUV then sped up in the fast lane to their left. Pedro could see the end of the barrel of the shotgun, slightly protruding from the passenger window.

"Erika, see the shotgun?"

"Check," Erika said looking at the SUV speeding toward them from their left.

"Blast them through your window," Wallace said.

As the SUV started to pull up next to them, a man wearing a black fedora hat and sunglasses leveled his shot gun, preparing to shoot Pedro.

Erika turned to her left and shot Davenport's assassin through the window three times in the face, snapping his head backward each time.

The SUV veered out of control and overturned on the grass between the westbound and eastbound lanes of the highway.

The white Chevrolet rammed their Rover from behind.

"Duck!" shouted Pedro. Erika, Wallace and Pedro slipped down into their seats.

Davenport's thug sitting in the front passenger leaned out the window and fired into the back window of the Rover, showering the back seat with blue-green shards of glass.

"Mother fuckers!" Pedro shouted, "Hang on!" He slammed on the breaks.

The Chevy slammed into the back of their Rover, causing both the driver and the passenger to fall back into their seats when the air bags deployed.

Erika came up firing, shooting the driver in the face. The Chevy veered right and crashed into the guard rail.

"Stop the Rover," Wallace shouted.

Pedro pulled to the side of the highway and turned the engine off. Both Wallace and Erika got out the car.

"Cover me," Wallace told Erika.

The old detective walked to the white car, its engine smoking and radiator dripping. He took out one of his Glocks and finished off the two wounded men.

Chapter 33

By Nerisha Kemraj, Mark Kodama and L.T. Waterson

Pedro pulled up to the small rectangular guardhouse no

bigger than a large telephone booth. An electrified metal fence girded

Davenport's villa off Interstate 15 in the middle of the desert. It was an

oasis of colors, verdant trees, meticulously manicured lawns, orchids,

rare perfumed flowers and fountains. Security cameras were

everywhere.

Erika rolled down the rear seat driver's side window of her

Land Rover. The surprised guard spoke into the radio on his shoulder.

"Erika," he said, turning his head left to speak into the radio. Little

pieces of glass from the shattered back window covered the back seat

and floor of the vehicle.

"Send her through," came the reply.

The heavy wrought iron gate opened and the guard waved her

in.

The villa resembled an upscale gated suburban community

rather than a private mansion, with its straight newly paved asphalt

main road, large leafy trees and Spanish-**style** ranch houses. Pedro

pulled up to the front entrance of Davenport's residence, a three-story

hacienda with a colonnade adjoining it **to** living quarters for the guards.

Three security guards dressed in suits and wearing mirrored aviator sunglasses met them at the entrance. "She's here with Wallace and another man," the security chief Jimmy said into his radio attached to his shoulder.

The huge bronze door was a replica of Rodin's Gates of Hell. Erika, Wallace and Pedro accompanied by the three security men, entered the residence. Two men stood guard at the hallway with their assault rifles ready.

Jimmy brought Erika to a private room while Wallace and Pedro waited in the vestibule. He closed the door behind him and stood guard outside.

Erika made a call. "Davenport," Erika said into her cell phone.

"Erika, my dear. My attorney Colton has been trying to get in contact with you," the voice responded. "I will soon be joining you with my entourage. It will be good to see you again."

"Don't do anything funny. Those four Luka Brasis you sent to ambush us sleep with the fishes. Switch on the news. See the results for yourself."

Davenport turned to the news. **The** wreckage of the car chase **was** being carried on all channels.

"What do you want?" Davenport asked.

"Don't be such a hard ass, James. I have Wallace. You can have him. Do you have my money for me?"

"You overestimate your importance to me, Erika. Your last mission was hardly a resounding success, now was it?"

"Failure? It was not a failure. You just beat me to it. Santini had **a** lot of damaging evidence on you. I was **trying** to retrieve it but no, you screwed everything up."

Davenport's eyes widened.

"Use your head Davenport. He was working with the Interpol. Listening to everything."

The gears in Davenports head slowly turned. It could be true. But now, the temptation of Wallace within his reach was overwhelming.

"I want you to bring Wallace to the entrance of the abandoned building near Whiskey's Pete's at noon please, Erika."

"Bring my money. Double for Wallace being alive. Make it worth my trouble."

She hung up on him.

Sand stung their eyes as they left the Rover, walking the few steps to the abandoned building in the middle of nowhere. Davenport's men followed in two black SUVs. Treacherous mountains and red rock surrounded them. This was the valley of death. Erika took **the** Rover keys from Pedro.

"He's already here. We're walking into an ambush."

Pedro whispered to Wallace, "This is a set up."

Wallace nodded.

A Davenport security man dressed in a suit and mirrored sun glasses stood at the entrance, ushering them with a wave of his submachine gun. Four security men from the SUV followed.

Davenport swerved to greet them from an office chair, an unlit cigar in his hands. Two giant henchmen towered over him. Erika turned her gun on Wallace.

"There's your prize. I want my money."

"Straight down to business then. First, however, who is your companion? An introduction would be polite?"

"He will help me carry the cash to the car."

"Search them," Davenport said to his men.

"Stop!" Erika shouted. "You have Wallace. **Now, my** money."

Davenport turned to Wallace. "I have been looking forward to this day for a very long time, Wallace. My mother will finally have justice."

One of the men handed two brief cases filled with money to Erika. Then, it all happened fast.

A bullet whizzed past Erika. She drew her gun and shot one of Davenport's security men in the face.

Pedro shot the man with the submachine gun in the throat. Wallace shot a third man in the shoulder and fourth man in the chest.

One of **Davenport's** henchmen grabbed Erika's arm and she pistol whipped him in the head, forcing him backward.

Wallace grabbed Davenport and put a gun to his head.

"Tell them to stop shooting."

Davenport waved at his men to stop.

Erika grabbed the suitcases and the three made for the Land Rover with Davenport as their hostage.

Erika loaded the two brief cases in the Land **R**over and got into the driver's side.

Pedro opened the passenger door while Wallace held Davenport from behind.

There was a crack from a rifle from one of Davenport's men, Wallace fell backward hit in the left arm. Davenport broke free and ran toward the desert, but didn't get far. Wallace shot him in the back.

Police sirens wailed as Clark **County** police cars flooded onto **the** property. Erika sped away into the desert in the Land **R**over.

Lt. Dense and his team of detective pulled up in unmarked cars, gun drawn.

###

Erika abandoned her Land Rover at a public parking lot. She called a taxi as she glanced around ensuring she wasn't being followed. A new life across the ocean called out to her. She'd saved enough over the last few months. Enough to go home to her daughter.

She opened the locket she wore close to her heart. A picture of a little girl **with long dark** hair and **brown** eyes smiled back at her. *Chiara.* Her hair and eyes may have been Roman's but her face was all her mother's. Anyone would have mistaken Chiara for a little Erika.

"**All** aboard the MSC…" the speakers blared.

"I'm coming home, my angel. I'm coming home."

Erika watched the sun setting over the dark sea, as the ship departed.

Tomorrow began a new life.

Other Stories

Land of the Pharaohs
By Mark Kodama

I.

Big Mo Turner sat erect mounted on his chestnut horse under
a large oak tree atop a small hill. The overseer and former slave
watched slaves picking cotton on the Colonel's North Carolina
plantation. Big Mo - wearing an old wide-brimmed hat, gray cotton
shirt and faded blue Army pants and brown leather boots – occasionally
swatted away a horsefly as he leaned forward in his saddle, his white
assistant overseer also on his horse by his side.

Big Mo was Nat Turner's son, the Nat Turner that led the
largest slave revolt in American history, just 34 years earlier. Defeat
was everywhere in the air as General Sherman and his army relentlessly
chased was Gen. Joseph Johnston and his army northward. Confederate
Generals Lee recently surrendered the Army of Northern Virginia and
President Jefferson Davis was on the run.

Joshua, a black teenager, ran from the Big House to Big Mo and handed him a note. Big Mo read the note, then carefully folded the note and the tucked it into his cotton shirt pocket. He turned to his white assistant. Big Mo pointed to the field and told his assistant to order everybody to gather at the Big House.

"The Colonel wants to speak to everyone," Young Joshua said, expectantly looking up to Big Mo.

"Well," Big Mo said looking down at Joshua from his horse.

"Is that all you have to say?" Young Joshua asked.

"There ain't nothin' else to say," Big Mo replied.

"Gen'ral Lee and Gen'ral Johnston surrendered," Young Joshua said. "And Jeff

Davis is on the run. The war is over. We free."

Big Mo looked down at Joshusa for a moment. "Oh yeah. We are far from the Promised Land. We are just a gett'n started."

"I'm glad slavery is dead," said the assistant overseer. "Our peculiar institution ain't never made no sense to me. Why would anyone want to work for nuth'in anyways? You have to force someone to do so. And for the white people who didn't own slaves ain't they poor nuf anyways without having to compete against rich people who do not have to pay their workers.

"Any person with spirit has to have their spirit shattered. And any one that is docile becomes more docile. And free whites no longer want to do the work slaves do. The whole system is brutal and inhumane and lacks sense.

"Go to Ohio for instance. No man is too proud to do a job. And look at their economy – the way they live compared to the way we live."

"I reckon," Big Mo said.

The assistant overseer tipped his hat to Big Mo and then rode his horse to the Cotton field.

"You ain't gonna stay here with the Colonel is you?" Joshua said. "You Moses. I thought you supposed to lead us to the Promised Land. That's what the preacher says the Bible say."

"Well, that Moses is a different Moses," Big Mo said.

"What are you gonna do?" Joshua asked.

"What's right for me," Big Mo said.

The field hands walked passed Big Mo and Joshua toward the plantation house.

"Everyone is gathering at the big house," a field hand said. "The Colonel has something to say."

"I will take my own sweet time,' Joshua said. "I free now.
"What is freedom if you can't choose to take your sweet time, hurry or
not go at all?"

"Are you strong? Big Mo said. "If you not strong, can you
become strong? If the answers to both questions are no, then ain't never
a gonna be truly free. If you already strong then you are already free."

The slaves returning from the cotton field sang:

Wade in the water,
Wade in the water children,
Wade in the water,
God's gonna trouble the water.

The Colonel - dressed in a handmade suit and white gloves –
stood in the shadows of the porch, concealing his face. He announced
that they were now free. They could stay at the plantation if they
wanted or leave. He said he could not pay anyone now but he would
feed and clothe those who stayed and would pay them when he was
able.

Afterward, the Colonel asked Big Mo to join him in his study
in the Big House for a drink. When Big Mo entered his study, the
Colonel was sitting at his desk with his back to Big Mo. When the
Colonel turned, his face and hands were badly disfigured by fire. He

limped to the cherry wood table in his office and poured two glass
tumblers full of apple brandy, handing one to Big Mo . "Cheers.'the
Colonel said. "Can't feel my hands. Damn fires."

He asked Big Mo to remain at the plantation and to continue
to run it. Big Mo would receive a piece of land. The Colonel recalled
their service together in the Confederate Army. He thanked Big Mo for
saving his life at the Battle of the Wilderness. If Big Mo had not carried
him from the fight, he would have burned to death in the fire. The
Colonel had been shot in the leg and could not stand.

The Colonel said that he owned slaves as his daddy and
granddaddy did. They were good hard working family men –
Christians. He asked Big Mo if owning slaves was wrong. Big Mo
answered his question with a question. "Would you trade places with
me? If you answer yes, then you are a fool. If no, then I think you
understand."

"Life is strange," Big Mo said. "Slavery is filled with
contradictions that make no sense. You see I have two arms, two legs,
two eyes, nose and a mouth just like you. We are not much different.
Yet you are considered a man and I property.

"You may be the only friend I have. Yet you have kept me in chains until now. And I fought in a war to keep myself in chains through my own freedom is what I most wanted."

Big Mo said he has other plans. He wanted to search for his mother and siblings in Southampton, Virginia. He dressed in his Confederate uniform for protection.

"Mo, have you ever heard of the Myth of Sisyphus," asked the Colonel.

"Can't say I have," Big Mo said.

"Well, Sisyphus was the mythical king of the Thebans," the Colonel said. "He was infamous for his cleverness and trickery.

"At the end of his life, the Greek gods sent Death to take him to the underworld," the Colonel said. "When Death came with his manacles, Sisyphus asked him to show him how the manacles worked. After Death put the manacles on himself, Sisyphus took away his key and kept Death as his prisoner.

"After that no one could die. An angry Ares, the god of war, demanded Zeus, the king of the gods, do something. So Zeus sent his son Hermes, the messenger god, to free Death. Hermes freed Death and led Sisyphus to the underworld. The gods punished Sisyphus by making him roll a heavy stone up a mountain every day to watch it roll down again.

"The next day he again would have to roll the stone up the mountain and so on throughout eternity. He was condemned to live a meaningless afterlife in punishment for his living a meaningless life.

"Sometimes I think I'm Sisyphus. I spent my life trying to build this plantation from swampland, enduring the ups and down of the weather and changing economy. Then the war comes. I barely survive the war, only to come to my plantation destroyed by the union army. And I do not do this for myself. My plantation is like a ship at sea. Everyone on that ship is dependant upon that ship for sustenance. So my family, my workers and all my slaves and all of their families are dependent upon this plantation. "

"Do you know what I think?" asked Big Mo.

"What do you think?" asked the Colonel.

"Sisyphus must be happy," Big Mo said.

"What do you mean," asked the Colonel.

"Life is a rebellion against fate," Big Mo said. "And rebellion gives life meaning."

The Colonel handed Big Mo money for his journey. "Not much, but it is all I have," he said. "Good luck Mo. Fortune favors the brave."

Joshua, a teenager without family, wanted to join Big Mo on his journey to Southampton. "Where are we going, Big Mo?" he asked.

"No where."

"You look like you are leaving," Joshua said. "I want to go whicha."

"I am leaving," Big Mo said. "But not with you."

"Why not?"

"I didn't invite you," Big Mo said.

"I can help you," said Joshua.

"Don't need no help," Big Mo said. "I travel light."

"I will help you."

"It may be dangerous," Big Mo said. "I move faster on my own."

"I will help you."

"Okay then meet me in two hours at Liberty Road."

"Where are we going?"

"Land of the Pharaohs," Big Mo said.

When Joshua arrived at Liberty Road, Big Mo is not there. Two old black men sitting on a porch in homemade wood rocking chairs told Joshua Big Mo left an hour ago. Joshua ran to catch up.

II.

Big Mo and Joshua came to the small town of Golgotha, a town in the midst of a local election. A flyer of the local Sheriff Flay announcing his re-election campaign was displayed in the store window.

Two black Union soldiers, a sergeant and a private, stood on the stone sidewalk in front of the stor. The private bated Big Mo and asked him for which side he fought. The sergeant, however, restrained the younger man.

"Don't mess with a guy like that. That man is a survivor. And dangerous."

" I faced tough men in battle."

"Your pride will kill you some day. Don't go looking for trouble. Trouble will find you sure enough anyways."

Big Mo and Joshua enter the town's general store. A timid white clerk with thick glasses and hunched shoulders stood behind the counter.

Big Mo gathered butter, sugar, eggs, buttermilk, salt, pepper, flour and cornmeal.

The clerk cleared his throat and said in an overly loud voice: "We don't serve no niggah's here."

Big Mo stared him down as Joshua fidgeted. "We ain't no niggahs. You must be mistaken. Look at my uniform."

The clerk in fear looks timidly at the ground. "I see. Well that will be three dollars and twenty cents then."

Rose-fingered dawn rose with the sun behind the tree line. Mist veiled the brook carrying the cold mountain water to the sea. After Big Mo finished reading his newspaper the North Star, he fed it into the fire. Big Mo cooked trout and cornbread in two pans on the campfire.

"All you really need to cook trout is salt, pepper and oil and a hot fire," Big Mo said.

If you cook the fish too long, it becomes to rubbery; too short and its raw. If you cook it just right it is tender, flaky and flavorful. Life is like cooking. Timing is everythin'.

"And the mos' satisfying pleasures in life are often times the mos' simple pleasures. The trees, the river, the food and the smell of the fire – life gets no better than this. It's ready. Eat up."

"Ain't you gonna say grace before eatin'," Joshua asks.

"You can say it for yourself if you want," Big Mo said.

"Don't you believe in God?" Joshua asks.

"Four days a week, yes," Big Mo said. "Three days no."

"Why don't you believe in God all the time?' Joshua asks.

"Because you can't prove He exists," Big Mo said.

"The preacher says 'who could create all this beauty but God?'" Joshua said. "That is proof that God exists."

"Why can't nature have created nature?" Big Mo said.

"Without God there would be no morality," Joshua said.

"Why is that?" Big Mo said.

"Ain't you afraid of being cast into the fiery pit of hell?"

"If God exists, don't you think He would want you to believe in Him because He exists and not because you are scared not to believe?"

"Well, then why do you believe in God for four days," Joshua asked.

"Well, because you can't prove God doesn't exist," Big Mo said.

"You are a strange man," Joshua said.

"No, I think for myself," Big Mo said. "I am my own man. I think people are strange when they don't have the confidence to believe in themselves."

Later, after they finished breakfast, Big Mo poured water on the fire.

"Where did you learn to read?" Joshua asks.

"From my daddy," Big Mo said.

"How did your daddy know how to read?" Joshua asked.

"He was a negro preacher," Big Mo said.

"Who taught him how to read?

"He taught himself how to read," Big Mo said.

"That's a miracle," Joshua said.

"So they said," Big Mo said.

Later that evening, two local white men - an older man and a younger man.- appeared at their camp.

"Hey boy, what are you two doin,' camping in our woods and eating fish from our river," the older man said.

"This is God's country," Big Mo said. "It ain't your fish."

"You are niggah," the older man said. "Show some respect. You can't talk to me like that. You know the rules. "

"We don' want any trouble," Big Mo said. "Push on ol' man."

The older man pointed his shotgun at Big Mo. "Boy, get down on the ground." He turns to the younger man whose grinning. "Tie them up."

When the younger man bended down to tie Big Mo. Big Mo knocked him to the ground and put a knife to his throat.

"Now lower your shotgun or your young friend is a dead man," Big Mo said. "Now throw it over there on the grass."

"Don't harm my son," the older man said.

The old man throws his gun away. Big Mo then rushed him, knocking him to the ground. He then slit his throat. "The first shall be last," Big Mo told him as he killed him.

The younger man tried to run away. Big Mo tackled him. Big Mo then he held a knife to his throat.

"Have mercy," the young man said.

"Too late," Big Mo said. "You should have thought of that before."

Before Big Mo kills him, he said. "And the last shall be first."

Big Mo limped toward Joshua. "Damn, I turned my ankle," he said.

"Oh, Lordy," Joshua said. "God is going to punish us now."

"Boy, wipe those thoughts from you mind," Big Mo said. First, there ain't no God. Second, if there is a God, He does not live down here on earth. Do not think so hard. Just do.

"Now give me a hand," Big Mo said. "The white folks do live here on earth and the sheriff will certainly punish us."

"We done wrong Big Mo,"Joshua said.

"What wrong did we do?" Big Mo said. "We were just defending ourselves. What real choice did we have? We chose life. Nothin wrong with that. Even insects understand that."

"Damn, I've never met a man like you before Big Mo," Joshua said.

"I'm just a man like every other man," Big Mo said. "We are in great danger. We need to be smart now."

"You the boss," Joshua said.

"You are damn right," Big Mo said. "So do everything I say."

" Those white folks deserved what they got," Joshua said.

"No one deserves it and we all have it coming to us," Big Mo said. "Now let's get rid of these bodies."

Big Mo turned to Joshua. "I did not make this world," Big Mo said. " I just deal with it as it is."

They tied large stones to the bodies and threw them into the river. They camprf for a couple days until Big Mo could walk again. When Big Mo and Joshua set out again, they eere stopprf by Sheriff Flay who was looking for the two missing locals. Sheriff Flay had a "hunch" that Big Mo and Joshua had something to do with the disappearance.

"Sometimes we are all that stand between order and anarchy," Sheriff Flay told his deputies. "God may determine what is right and wrong. But it still must be enforced by man with all his imperfections here on earth."

"If not for the sovereign, it would be a war of all against all," said Flay said. "Life for all would solitary, poor, nasty, brutish and short. Freedom requires restraint for there is no freedom without law.

"Without restraints man is nothing but a beast," Flay said. "If you throw money into the mix, man is the very worst of the beasts."

Sheriff Flay threatened to torture Big Mo. Big Mo coolly replied that if he tortures him he better kill him. When Big Mo takes off his shirt, Sheriff Flay notices his powerful build and askrf him about his scars.

Big Mo tells him about his war scars. When Sheriff Flay asks him about bite scars, Big Mo said he got them fighting a gator. When Flay asked him what happened, Big Mo showed Flay his knife and said "I killed him."

Flay said "out of respect to your service to the cause, I will not harm you." He, however, tried to whip a confession from Joshua who remained silent.

Flay turned to his deputy. "Mersault, take care of him."

"You did good," Big Mo tells Joshua. "I will teach you how to survive and see the world as it really is. Innocence is a luxury for the sheltered. For us it can me only death. There is no God or at least one that hears our cries. The world is indifferent to your struggles. Safety lies only in yourself.

"If there is any rule to this world, it is the rule of self preservation," Big Mo said. "Man is a beast. And even a fox caught in the trap will gnaw off its own leg to survive."

###

Big Mo carried Joshua to a rough cabin at the edge of the woods. A black woman about the age of 30 answers the door. Her name is Diotima. Big Mo told her that the boy was hurt and asked for her help. She opened the door and helped carry Joshua to her own bed.

"Aren't you gonna ask who we are?" asked Big Mo.

"Do you need my help?." Diotima asked.

"Yes," Big Mo said.

"Then I do not need to know," she said.

"Are you afraid of the law?" Big Mo asked.

"There are higher laws," she replied.

The next morning, Big Mo thanked her and began to leave. Diotima asked him where he was going. Big Mo replied "I ain't got no blood ties to the boy. He ain't no kin of mine."

"You don't need no blood ties to be bound to another," Diotima replied: "He's your friend and he looks up to you. You can't abandon him. You have a duty to him."

"I am in a hurry to get to home to find my ma, brother and sister," Big Mo said. "And we do not really have friends in life."

"You have waited 35 years to see them," Diotima said. "Whether you wait *now* or not, ain't gonna make no difference. Your family is either there or not there. "

"Life is a solitary journey," Big Mo said. "Who can you really count on anyways? In the end, your life is only your own."

"I'm sorry life has treated you with a rough hand," she said. "But we all have to endure our share of unfairness."

"I don't feel sorry for myself," Big Mo said. "So don't feel sorry for me either."

" It is up to each person to make this a better world," she said.

"Hope sometimes is all we have. A man without hope does not belong to the future. You can't leave the boy. The boy needs you *now*. I speak the truth."

" There is no truth, only truths," he said.

" Don't confuse solitude with freedom. You are a stranger – unto others and even unto yourself. No man is an island, entirely unto himself." Diotima said. " We all need each other. The boy can't be used as some means for your escape. He is a person just like you."

" I can't afford self delusions," Big Mo said. "I see the world as it is. We are only as strong as ourselves. We don't need others if we are strong. And I know of no man stronger than me."

"We all are born and then die," Diotima said. "So in a sense life is futile. We must do something between our birth and death to make our lives meaningful. We must therefore at least make our own life mean something. We must at the very least leave this world a better place than we found it."

Diotima picked flowers and herbs in her garden. When Joshua walked into the garden, Diotima smiled.

"Well, look at you," Diotima said. "You are a strong young man."

"Yes, ma'm," Joshua said.

"Do you like flowers Joshua?" Diotima asked.

"No," Joshua said. "Flowers are for girls."

"Are they?" Diotima said. She smiled. "Smell this."

Joshua smelled the flower.

"Don't they smell good?" she said. "Don't they look good?"

"Yes, Ma'm," Joshua said.

"Then you do like flowers," Diotima said. "It is not unmanly to like beautiful things. It is quite natural to love the things made by God."

"Yes ma'm," Joshua said.

"You see I grew these flowers from seeds," Diotima said. " I planted the seed in the soil. I watered the plants. I weeded the garden."

"Yes, ma'm," Joshua said.

"You see flowers are miracles," Diotima said, bending down and smelling. "Any one in search of miracles need not look any further than a flower. If you watch carefully, you will see that God is always teaching us something."

"Can I ask you something?" Joshua said.

"Of course," Joanna said.

"Are you negro?" he asked.

"Why do you ask?" she said.

"Because you look negro and you don't look negro," he said.

"Does it matter?" she asked.

"I 'spose it doesn't," he said.

"I am from everywhere and I am from nowhere," she said. "I am black. I am white. I am American Indian. I am one of God's children. That's what is important. We all are."

"Yes, ma'm," he said.

"The most important thing is that you judge all people as individuals," she said. "Because all people are individuals, each with their own characters and peculiarities."

"Well, I judge no one," Joshua said. "Because I am no one."

"Don't ever say that, Joshua," Diotoma said. "There will always be plenty of people who will try to make you feel like a nobody. If you listen to them, you will be a nobody. And you will have nobody to blame but yourself."

"Thank you for giving us shelter," Big Mo said. "Diotima, you are a beacon of light in a dark world. Here is payment."

"I didn't do it for payment," Diotima said.

"That is all the more reason for accepting my gratitude," Big Mo said.

"No keep it," Diotima said. "You may need it."

"No, please take it," Big Mo said. "You need it."

"Your gratitude is payment enough," she said. "I won't take your money. I just wanted to help because it was the right thing to do.

"God always provides," she said. "Ask and ye shall receive."

III.

After Joshua recovered, Big Mo and Joshua set out for Southampton County. When they crossed into Southampton County, they came upon a dried head of one of the black men on a post. He was killed in the Southampton Insurrection 34 year ago. It was a large head with a large scar from his right eye to his chin.The sign said Blackhead Signpost Road.

Big Mo looks up to the head and tears stream down his cheeks. "So they killed you too," he said to the head. "I thought you were the one man they couldn't kill."

"Will … Will . . . I thought they could never kill you," Big Mo said.

Later, Big Mo told Joshua that General Will was one of the leaders of the Southampton Insurrection. Big Mo also told Joshua that Big Mo was the son of Nat Turner, the leader of the largest slave revolt in the history of the United States.

"My father led the army, but Will and Hark did the killing," Big Mo told Joshua. "In a revolution, someone has to do the killing.

"And they did it was axes," he said. "Men, women and children. even infants. It was terrible. You can see the fear in the eyes of the men you knew all your life. You could their last breath as life ebbed from the eyes. Perhaps there is an afterlife after all. Only they know for certain.

"One moment they are alive like you and me. Then they are dead – no more alive than a fallen tree or piece of meat. There is nothing good about killing another person.

"By the time the revolt was put down, we killed nearly 60 local men, women and children. My father was caught a month later. Those that had been captured, including my father, were tried and hung. They made a purse from his skin and kept on of his hands as a souvenir.

"Hundreds of innocent blacks, slaves and freemen, were murdered by vigilantes in the bloodbath that followed. Because I was a child at the time, I was shipped out of state and sold again as a slave."

Night was falling and it began to rain. Big Mo and Joshua sought shelter at a rough cabin in the woods. Big Mo knocked on the door. A black woman about 50 answered the door.

When the woman answered the door, her guys grew big with surprise. "Oh my God. Mo is that you? Is that really you?"

"Delilah," Big Mo replied. "Yes. It's me. And I'm home."

Delilah became angry. "God damn you." She slapped his face. "Your daddy killed my daddy and brother."

"They made their own choice," Big Mo said.

"Your father mislead them," she said. "He had no special powers."

"They were men, free to decide for themselves," he said.

She then turned her back. "You and the boy can stay here until the rain passes. Then you must move on."

That night Big Mo dreamed. It was the final battle of the insurrection. Nat Turner was in the center like the Great King. Will was by his side, captured musket in hand. The last time he saw Will through the smoke and haze he was firing the musket.

The white militia men began their attack. Smoke was all around. Bullets whizzed all around. People were getting shot all around. The black rebels were greatly outnumbered. A few were drunk on apple brandy. As the militia men closed all around, the black army broke and ran.

"God, have you forsaken us?" Nat Turner said as those around him were shot.

Big Mo stood among the few who stood at their position. Surrounded he and the dozen who held their positions surrendered.

The dead and dying lay in the grass.

In the morning, Big Mo took an empty bucket of water to the spring and then brought back.

When he returned, Delilah was starting a fire in the stove. "I'm sorry," she said. "You and the boy can stay here as long as you want. Do you want some coffee?"

"What happened to Momma?" Big Mo asked.

"Gone," Delilah said.

"Dead?" Big Mo said.

"Did I say that? Delilah said.

"Then what?" Big Mo asked.

"Gone," she said. After your daddy was captured, they tortured Cherry. By the time they were finished there was no skin left on her back. Finally, she showed them papers your father left with her."

"Afterwards, she disappeared with your brother and sister. They said they were transported out of state and sold in Mississippi."

IV.

Big Mo and Joshua were at the Giles Reese farm. Big Mo was sitting amongst scattered logs in what was a rough cabin.

"This is where I grew up," Big Mo said. "Used to hunt coons and possums here with my lil' brother."

"Noth'in left," Joshua said.

"Jus' ghosts," Big Mo said. "And memories."

"My daddy once baptized a white man in the river. He was a troubled but good man: an overseer on one of the plantations.

"When my daddy baptized him in the river all the people turned out. The black folk were there to cheer. The white folk were there to jeer.

###

Big Mo and Joshua were at a pond. Water oaks and cypresses grew from the water and the banks. Lily pads floated in the water. Flies buzzed.

"This is where it all started," Big Mo said. "When my daddy arrived, General Hark and

Nelson the conjurer were roasting a pig. Will the Executioner was sitting on his haunches. His ax was at his side. Henry, Sam and Jack were drinking apple brandy. All seemed like just yesterday. There was so much hope. All seemed possible."

###

It is August 21, 1831, Cabin Pond, Virginia. Nat Turner, 31, a small charismatic man arrives.

"The preacher is here," said Nelson the conjurer.

"Brother Nat," Hark said.

The men embraced.

Nat then embraced Nelson, Henry and Sam.

"All is ready," Nat said. "Judgment Day is here."

"God is with us," Nelson said. "Since God is with us, who can stand against us? I can see the future. I see success."

"Who are you?" Nat said to Will.

"I am Will," he said.

"He is a good man, Nat," Hark said.

"How come you are here?" Nat asked Will.

"My life is worth no more than everyone else's," Will said. "I'm here to win our freedom or die."

"Well, it is now time," Nat said. "God has ordered us."

"Amen, preacher," Henry said.

"With God on our side, we cannot lose," Nelson said.

"There is only seven of us," Jack said. "This makes no sense. It will only lead to our deaths. And bring the full wrath of the white folk upon our heads. And how are we to murder innocent women and children?"

"More will join," Hark said. "We must believe in ourselves. If the white folk treat us like animals we do not have to behave like men. This is a life and death struggles and our odds are long enough already.

"The militia is out of town. We will strike quickly without warning, " Nat said. "Others will join us. We will be in Jerusalem before they can organize."

"How do you know?" Jack said.

"The way has been prepared," Nat said. "The hand of the Lord is upon us. God will strengthen us. Are you questioning God? Did not the Lord say 'Seek ye the kingdom of heaven and all things shall be added unto you.' We shall slay our oppressors with their own weapons."

"Don't be afraid though briers and thorns are all around you and scorpions surround you.

"Jehovah commanded 'The end is upon you and I will unleash my anger against you. I will judge you according to your conduct and I will repay you for all your detestable practices.

"I saw a vision of white spirits and black spirits in the fight to the death," Nat said. "We must have faith. If we lose confidence in God and ourselves we are as good as dead."

"Believe in the prophet," Nelson said. "He sees the future. He controls the clouds. God speaks directly to him. God has commanded the prophet to lead his people in a great battle against slavery."

"Didn't you see the signs: the solar eclipse? Today, the sun turned green."

"Believe in the prophet," Henry repeated. "You do not need to reason. All you have to do is believe."

"I sees what I sees," Will said. "I hears what I hears. I touches what I touches. I believes in nothing else. You may control clouds. You may walk on water. I ain't gonna believe in nothin' I can't see myself.

"I ain't gonna believe in no God at leas' here on earth," he said. "On earth, we must take our own life in our own hands. You see mah ax? That's what I believe in.

"I will win my freedom or die," he said. "When I die I 'spect no pearly gates; no singin' angels. When I die, I 'spect only death.

"While I live I want to breath free air," he said. "I want to work when I want to work. I want to res' when I want to res. And I want to enjoy the fruits of my own labor."

"I want to judge for myself what is right and wrong," he said. "I don' want no one tellin' me what is right and what is wrong."

"White man starves you then whips you for steal'in his food. He sends you to the field 'fore the sun rises and then sends you home to your rough cabin after dark.

"He sells your chil'ren the same as his cows, pigs and chickens. He treats his mules better than you."

"God commands it," Sam said. "I'm tired of waiting for someone to free us. Let's free ourselves through our own courage. A slave who says yes to everything consents to his own suffering. Let my people go."

"There is nothin' we can do about it now anyways," Henry said. "The die has been cast. Our fate is our fate."

"Let the preachers pray and the philosophers think," Hark said. "We are in the Land of the Pharaohs. All roads lead to death. I choose to die fighting for our freedom rather than to live in slavery.

"Whatever they can do, they cannot take away our right to choose. By fighting, I choose life."

"A better day is coming," Nat said.

The men began to sing together:

When Israel was in Egypt's land:
Let my people go,
Oppress'd so hard they could not stand,
Let my People go.
Go down, Moses,
Way down in Egypt's land,
Tell old Pharaoh,
Let my people go.

"We met Nat and the rebels in the yard of the Travis farm,"
Big Mo said. "It was the farm where Nat worked. It was 2 a.m. and all
was quiet. We proceeded to the cider press where all drank except
Nat."

"Now, it is time to make good all your valiant boasts," Nat
said. Nat and Will looked at each other in the eyes. Will raised his ax
and then laughed. Nat looked away.

Hark lifted the ladder and set it against the chimney. Nat
climbed the ladder to a second story window. He opened the window
and silently entered the house. He opened the front door and let us in.

"The work is now open to you," Nat said to Will.

The men went to the master bedroom. Nat lifted his hatchet and hit his master Joseph Travis in the head with his hatchet, wounding him.

"Sally!" Travis called to his wife. Will moved Nat aside and killed Travis with his ax then killed Sally.

The rebels then killed the overseer and Sally's son Putnam. Jack said he was too sick to continue. The rebels forced him to get up and follow them.

"Can't we let him be?" Sam asked.

"Show no pity," Hark said. "We must be strong."

The men took all the weapons and horses. After they left, the men remembered that they forgot to kill the infant. Will and Henry returned to the house and killed the baby.

The rebels killed Sal Francis and then killed Piety Reese and her son William at their farm. They then killed Elizabeth Turner, her friend Mrs. Newsome and the overseer Hartwood Peebles. By the next day, they had killed 60 men, women and children.

Many slaves voluntarily joined the insurgency. Some that did not join were taken at gunpoint. They were also joined by free blacks. One slave who refused to join had his ankles cut so he could not walk.

"Davy, does not want to come," Sam said.

"If he does not come, kill him" Nat said.

"We are already outnumbered," Hark said. "We need every

man we can get. It's power versus power. And we are not only fighting

for your lives we are fighting for the freedom of our people."

By the time, the rebels reached the Whitehead Plantation,

there were 15 men, nine on horseback. When they reached the

plantation, Richard, a young Methodist preacher was in the field with

his slaves.

"You, come here," Nat said.

The insurgents surrounded him. They began to chant "Kill

him! Kill him!"

"Please," Richard cried. "Why do you want to kill me?

"Ýe hypocrite," Nat said.

Will began to chop Richard to pieces.

"Please," Richard cried.

Will dragged Caty Whitehead, Richard's mother from the

house. "I don't want to live since you murdered all my children," she

told Will.

She looked into the eyes of Old Hubbard her servant.

Will then cut her head off with his ax, her blood spattered all over his face and arms. Her adult daughter Margaret screamed and in a panic runs in terror toward the woods.

Will looks at Nat and nods at him. Nat chased her down. He began to beat her with his blunt sword. He then picked up a wood fence post. He starts to beat her head with the heavy post. Her bloods and hair spatters all over his arm and face.

Old Hubbard, the family servant, said, there was no one left. In fact, he hid Harriett Whitehead and thereby saved her life. After the rebels left, Old Hubbard hid Harriett in the swamp.

At the Waller homestead, Waller's wife and two daughters and a group of school children were slaughtered. Waller survived by hiding in the weeds. One child survived by hiding in the chimney.

Sam stood alone weeping while other rebels drank apple brandy. When Nat saw him, he ordered him to get on his horse.

"We must be strong," Nat said.

The rebels killed John Barrow in hand to hand combat. They wrapped him in a quilt and left tobacco on his chest in respect for his valor.

"I'm sorry such a man had to die," Nat said.

At one homestead, Nat held his men back. "Those people think themselves no better than negroes," he said.

At the rebel army came upon new plantations and farm, many of them had been abandoned by their owners who now heard about the rebellion. When they came upon the Harris farm, only the slaves were there. By now, we had more than 40 men.

"You don't stand a chance," on slave Aaron told Nat. "If you knew how many armed white folks were at Norfolk you would have thought twice about attacking them."

"Do you want us to kill you?" Will asked.

"We are not afraid of you," Aaron said. "Violence does not equal strength. A man of peace is more powerful than a man of war. Your tyranny is not any better than the tyranny you are trying to replace."

"You should die many deaths," Will said.

"Let them be," Nat said.

At the Parker Plantation, the rebels and militia clashed. The fighting was inconclusive and several rebels were wounded. The rebels retreated after the militia was reinforced.

###

The rebels tried to march on Jerusalem, the county seat. But some of their numbers had deserted; others were too drunk to fight. In addition, some of their muskets were rusty and did not fire.

Meantime, the whites had organized and called for help. Reinforcements were arriving from Richmond, Norfolk and North Carolina.

Once they saw the bridges were well guarded, the rebels turned back.

The rebels camped that night at the Ridley Plantation. By dawn, half the rebels had deserted.

"What do you think will happen tomorrow?" asked Mo.

"We are all go'in to die," Will said.

Before marching out, the survivors sang their death song:

Michael row de boat ashore, Hallelujah,
I wonder where my mudder deh there,
See my mudder in de rock gwine home,
On de rock gwine home in Jesus's name,
Michael row a music boat.
Gabriel blow de trumpet horn . . . .

In the morning, Nat and the rebels moved to the Blount plantation to recruit more men. To their surprise, both the owners and their slaves fought back.

Hark was shot and badly wounded and captured. Another rebel was killed and a third captured.

After the rebel force retreated, they were attacked by the Greensville cavalry who attacked and dispersed their forces.

The revolution was over. Nat, Hark, and Sam were caught, tried and hung. Jack and Big Mo were caught, tried and sold out of state as a slave.

Will was killed in the fighting. Henry was caught by vigilantes and summarily executed.

V.

When they returned to the Delilah's cabin, it was nightfall. A a dozen white men arrested Big Mo and took him to the jail in Jerusalem.

"Are you Moses Turner?" asked the sheriff.

"That'd be me," Big Mo said.

"You are wanted in North Carolina for murder," the sheriff said.

Young Joshua escaped into the woods. He then returned to Golgotha and sought the help of Diotima.

###

"Give me your worst," Big Mo told Magistrate Judge Hawthorne. "You can't do anything to me that hasn't been done to me before."

"Castrate him," Magistrate Judge Hawthorne ordered. "He's an animal. And so he shall be treated like an animal."

"What about my rights?" Big Mo said.

"Here in this room behind these closed doors you have no rights but the rights I grant you," Magistrate Judge Hawthorne said.

"He's already been castrated," the guard said.

"Do you see this skull," Magistrate Judge Hawthorne asked Big Mo. He handed him a skull that looked as much as a ram as a man. "This is the head of your Daddy.

"After we hung him, we skinned him, made grease of his flesh and his skin into a leather purse.

"Give him such a beating that he will never come back," Magistrate Judge Hawthornes said.

The sheriff of Southampton County tried to deliver Big Mo to Sheriff Flay chained to the back of a wagon. But Big Mo escaped killing the driver and the guard. The driver was found with a broken neck. The guard had his throat cut.

Sheriff Flay found Bog Mo and Joshua at Diotima's cabin. The sheriff tried to arrest them but they refused to surrender.

Sheriff Flay had a dozen men surround the cabin.

Big Mo, Diotima and Joshua armed with rifles held out for five days.

###

"We've got to break out tonight," Big Mo said. "We're almost out of food, water and bullets. If we are captured, we are as good as dead."

"There is no moon tonight," Diotima said.

"Jus' follow me," Big Mo said. "We'll head for the woods and then cut to the river.

If we get separated make for the river."

A gun fight broke out. They ran toward the river but Diotima was shot in the back and was bleeding badly.

"Let me be," Diotima told them. "Go on. I'm dying anyways. I'm slowing you down."

###

By the time Sheriff Flay and his men found Diotima the sun had risen.

"Kill her," Flay shouted.

"She's a woman," Mersault said.

"She's a niggah," Flay said. "Finish her off."

"You can kill me but you can never destroy me," Diotima said.

Diotima closed her eyes. Mersault stuck his the barrel of his revolver into the back of her head. A crack of gun fire echoed across the valley. Mersault fell dead. The pistol fells in front of Diotima. She

picks up the gun.

Flay ducked behind a tree and his remaining men laid on the

ground.

"Big Mo, I know that's you, " Flay said. "Surrender. You and

the boy have no chance."

Flay motioned his men to move forward toward the river.

Another crack. Another one of Flay's men fell dead.

Another man ran toward the trees. Another crack. He was hit

in the shoulder.

Another man runs. Another crack. This time Big Mo misses.

Flay shots Big Mo as he fired, wounding him badly in the

torso. Flay ducked behind the tree. He turns and sees Diotima with her

pistol aimed at his head. "Oh, Lord," he said.

Diotima shoots him in the head, killing him. She then dies.

Flay's men rushed Big Mo. Big Mo shoots one man dead. The

rest of the men dive for cover.

Big Mo is mortally wounded. "You need to run," he rasps.

"I can't leave you," Joshua said.

"I'm a dead man," Big Mo said. "Now go."

By the time, the remaining deputies reached Big Mo.he was

dead.

Meanwhile, Joshua escaped across the river and turned north.

The Red Velvet Cupcake Murders
By Mark Kodama
Inspired by "A Taste of Friendship" by Shawn Klimek
And used with his permission.

I.   The Condo

It was the greatest birthday party ever: raucous singing, lunatic

dancing, and heavy drinking. Hermann, the neighbor below me,

repeatedly banged his ceiling with the end of a broom stick handle and

pounded on my door, yelling at me to hold it down or he would call the

cops. What a party! What a pity! I was the only one there.

Head throbbing and nauseated from a massive hangover, my

reflection stared back at me in the blank living room television: a

scraggy middle-aged fool dressed in a ridiculous party hat, teddy bear

onesie and foam slippers. Last night, I defiantly sang happy birthday to

myself as tears rolled down my face.

I prepared my homemade remedy of ginger and honey tea foe

hangovers. When I opened the refrigerator door for ginger, it was all

still there – the hors d'oeuvres, pepperoni pizza, chicken enchiladas and the clam dip. Melted wax from the candles shined on the untouched birthday cake. I had wasted all my considerable charm in a noble effort to befriend these unworthy, ungrateful neighbors. "What a bunch of losers," I said aloud then ran to the toilet and vomited.

Peering through the peephole of my front door, I unlocked the two dead bolts and the chain and opened the door to get my newspaper. But what was this? A colorful gift box on my newspaper. I laid the newspaper and gift box on the kitchen table.

Thankfully, the newspaper was untouched. Fernando's dog used to tear apart my morning paper. I spread laxative on it – killing the dog. I did not intend to kill the dog; but only wanted to teach him a lesson. Boy, was Fernando and his American girlfriend upset. I could hear them crying through the door. I grieved as much as the next person. Fernando – a baker at a donut shop - should have taken better care of his dog. Now, Fernando has a new puppy.

In my defense, I warned him about the newspaper. He only said "*No hablo Ingles.*" People should not come to this country and not speak English. Still I slipped a party invitation under his door. What is done and done. People should let bygones be bygones. I made the chicken enchiladas for him.

Since Fernando could not read his invitation, I drew a cake, party hat, balloons, streamers and confetti. I even drew his dead dog happily frolicking at the party with x's where his eyes should have been. Even if Fernando did not understand the party invitation his American girlfriend would be able to figure it out. She was a pretty girl with a gap tooth, about half his age. She often times wore her county animal shelter uniform while visiting him.

The kettle whistle blew. I poured the boiling water into my mug and let it steep. Maybe the gift giver could not make it to the party. This was his way of saying thanks for reaching out. I removed the ribbon and wrapping paper. Inside the box was a single red chocolate velvet cupcake with a sweet cream cheese butter icing, dusted with cocoa. The icing with white with a red and blue balloons and sprinkles on top. Very artistic. I peeled off the paper liner. The cupcake was soft and moist to the touch. It had an inner cream cheese vanilla filling. I alternately sipped my tea and nibbled the cupcake savoring the sweet, velvety chocolate that melted in my mouth.

Where was that missing note? Perhaps, my new friends were Dick and Ethel Hetherington – the old crippled couple. Old people are quite forgetful.

The old pharmacist smelled like urine and menthol cough drops. Ethel's cheap perfume sometimes concealed his embarrassing smell. She must have bathed in it. Unlike most people, I do not blame old people for being stinky.

I wanted to greet them – Dick in his wheelchair. But I had to hold my breath every time I saw them. They should be more considerate, using the stairs instead of the elevator. Ethel could exercise her arthritic knees and the taxi driver would appreciate the extra tip for carrying the wheelchair up and down the stairs. I attached a thought-provoking DVD to their invitation written in large print about euthanasia that I slipped under their front door.

What about the recipe? The secret ingredient of that velvet cupcake was possibly love. Maybe my new friend was the divorcee, Nora Smithfield. Nora wore younger women's dresses several sizes too small. Her pudding body and double chin jiggled as she moved. She squeezed her big feet into her garishly red high-heeled shoes.

Sometimes, a faded flower like that relies upon the kindness of strangers. That's one thing about me – I am a kind person. When she moved in to the building she asked about rats. "I hate rats," she shivered. I assured her that the building had no rats.

I looked at her love handles in a brotherly way, suggesting that she would be more attractive if she lost weight and wore dresses more suitable for someone her age. "Keep your opinions to yourself," she said.

Adapting and becoming more diplomatic, I encouraged her by saying "carrots" and "celery."

When she became annoyed, I said, "Moo."

When I personally delivered her invitation, I smiled. She forced a smile back. She claimed she had a date that night.

But it could not have been that old Nazi Hermann, the pest exterminator who lived below me. He was probably upset because I did not invite him.

I started to feel so strange. I began to wonder if I had been poisoned: I felt so restless, my head and jaw hurt and mouth tasted like metal. I saw flashing lights so. I called 911.

"Yes, I think I've been poisoned. . . . Is this going to cost me anything?"

"Name?"

"Walter . . . Walter Faff."

"Walter Fast. Where do you live?

"It's Faff, not Fast. I live at 5555 Beulah Road, Springfield, Virginia. Apartment 308."

"Mr. Fast, what symptoms are you experiencing?"

"I have a headache and my jaws are locking up," I said. "I am seeing flashes and my calves hurt."

"I see."

"Please hurry. I think I've been poisoned."

"Health insurance company?"

"Please hurry."

"Who are your insured by?"

"Who the hell cares? Please hurry."

"Mr. Fast, an ambulance is coming."

I undid the chain and unlocked the deadbolt and went to bed. My calves stiffened and then started to rhythmically jerk. My toes curled and my breathing became labored. I touched my ear lobes. They were burning hot.

Sirens wailed – faint and then louder. Everything went dark.

II.   Hospital

When I awoke I was in the emergency room. "Mr. Faff? I'm Dr. Jenkins," said the female voice. "Don't be scared. We're going to take good care of you."

A male nurse sheared the teddy bear onesie from my body in the dark room and then sponged my chest. I hurt all over.

"We think you have been poisoned," the woman's voice echoed. "We drew your blood. Your CK levels are off the charts."

"You are going feel a pinch," the nurse said and inserted the IV into my arm.

"We need to give put some fluids and medication," Dr. Jenkins said. "The phenobarbitol will control your convulsions and dantrolene will relax your muscles. We will give you morphine for your pain. How are you feeling?"

I wanted to speak but nothing came out. Dr. Jenkins patted my arm. "I won't lie to you. You are in a serious condition but we will get through it." She nodded to the male nurse. He shot something into my arm, putting me to sleep.

I awoke to a dark room. I was dressed in a hospital gown with an IV stuck in my right arm. A nurse came in and fluffed up the pillows behind my head.

"Mr. Faff, I'm Precious," she said with a Jamaican accent. "I am your nurse. We need to take your vitals."

"Hello, Mr. Faff," Dr. Jenkins smiled. "It looks like you are going to be okay." She wore no makeup on her face other than lipstick, a tiny piece hanging on her upper lip.

"Thank you," I croaked.

"You were poisoned by strychnine," she said. I watched the piece of lipstick bob up and down as she spoke. "Do you know how that might have happened?"

"The cupcake – the red velvet cupcake," I said.

She wrote it down. "You take it easy," Dr. Jenkins said. "We will talk some more later. The detectives want to see you."

I turned on the television with my remote. CNN. Something about President Trump. Election interference. Russian collusion. Porn star hush payments. Cover up. The light and sound made my head pound. I shut off the television.

My sister Mavis called me about my birthday. She was shocked that I had been poisoned by one of my neighbors. She urged me to sell my condo. "What is this world coming to when you can't even trust your neighbors?"

Mavis invited me for Thanksgiving dinner. I declined. "I know you and Lyndon have your differences. But he is your brother and you need to forgive and forget."

"I cannot talk much now," I said, barely above a whisper. "My jaw and lungs hurt."

"You take care of yourself," she said. "And be careful."

Inspector Harry Michalski and his partner Doug Brown interviewed me. Michalski was a big Pole with large hands and a shock of white hair. He had a craggy, pock-marked face and broken nose. He wore a cheap sports jacket that smelled like tobacco smoke. His breathe smelled like cigarettes, even through his hospital mask.

They wore sterile gowns since I was quarantined. They had been in my condo. It had been taped off as a crime scene. I told them about Pedro Alvarado – the Mexican doughnut baker with the dog. It turns out that Pedro Alvarado was his real name. I did not tell them about how I had accidently killed his dog by smearing my newspaper with laxatives. I did not want to confuse the issues.

I also told them about the retired pharmacist Hetherington and his wife Ethel, the divorcee Nora Smithfield and her hostility to men, and Hermann, the Nazi downstairs.

Inspector Michalski found strychnine in the gift box and the cupcake lining and the crumbs and icing they found on my onesie.

Michalski assured me he would find the criminal who did this to me. He gave me his business card. "We'll be in touch," he said. "Somebody wants you dead."

III.   The Workplace

When I returned to my job, I told my boss I had the flu. I worked as a copy editor at a trade weekly covering the federal government. My boss Bart Scholtz sat in his glass office.

"Faff, we have a number of stories in your queue," Scholtz said. He did not even say hello or shake my hand. He looked at me and then sprayed his hands with disinfectant.

"The new girl started while you were gone." Scholtz adjusted the pictures of his wife and children on his desk.

I smiled weakly. "Oh, what is her name?"

"Tina Bottoms," Scholtz said. "Pretty girl. Just out of journalism school." He licked his lips.

"Where did she graduate from?"

"I don't remember," he said impatiently. He looked at his watch. Then he looked at me his eyes narrowed.

"Oh, yes," I said. "Stories in my queue to edit."

Scholtz grimaced. I held out my hand.

He looked at my hand and then turned to his computer and began typing. He sprayed his hands again with disinfectant and rubbed his hands together.

I returned to my gray cubicle. I looked at the stories in my queue: Donald Trump, the Federal government, and federal workers on furlough and working without pay.

The new girl Tina Bottoms entered and sat down in her cubicle. She wore a freshly ironed red blouse with slacks. Her large leather bag slung over her right shoulder. It was 9:15 a.m. She was 15 minutes late.

Her music was so loud I could hear it through her head phones. She jumped when I tapped her shoulder. She turned, her false eye lashes blinking.

"Walter . . . . Walter Faff," I said holding my hand out toward her with a most friendly smile. She shook my hand, with her ice-cold hand.

"Oh, Tina . . . . Tina Bottoms," she said, trying to size me up.

"I'm one of the copy editors here," I said.

"Oh, that's nice," she said.

"What is your beat?" I asked.

"Oh, the postal service," she said.

"That's one of the most interesting assignments here."

"Really?"

"Yes. It will make you go postal!"

She laughed and held out her hand again.

"Nice meeting you," she smiled.

What a delicate young flower! I resolved there and then I would protect her against that pig Scholtz.

IV.   Neighbors

Upon returning home that night, I tried to make sense of it all. Who would want to poison me? I was the nicest and most caring person.

I surreptitiously watched my neighbors. My leading candidate was that Mexican Pedro Alvarado with his beady black eyes. As a baker he knew how to make cupcakes. And I had accidently killed his dog.

It could have been the Hetheringtons. Dick was a retired pharmacist. He certainly would know how to mix the poison. He probably resented that I sent him that DVD on euthanasia.

It could have been Nora Smithfield. She was a real black widow. She also hated rats. She must have known about rat poison.

Or perhaps it was that Nazi Hermann, an exterminator. And who knows what he did in Germany.

Inspector Michalski would get to the bottom of it. I had my locks changed and bought a .45-caliber pistol. You can never be too careful.

After several weeks. Michalski's partner Doug called me about my relationship with my neighbors, particularly with Pedro Alvarez. He was annoyed I did not tell him about Pedro's dead dog and the party invitation.

Months went by and nothing happened. Meanwhile, Scholtz and Tina were getting chummy. That old wolf told her some sad story about how unhappy he was with his wife and only stayed married to the harpy for the sake of the children. Why are women always so attracted to bad men?

Tina was good at wheedling information from people. But she needed to slow down and improve her writing. Break up her paragraphs and vary the lengths of her sentences. She was young. So I showed her some things. She was truly appreciative.

One day after work Tina asked me if we could go out to dinner together as friends. During dinner, she said she and that creep Scholtz were having an affair. She was confused because she was not that kind of a girl.

I told her that she should stop sleeping with that bastard Schlotz forthwith. He had done this over the years to several new female reporters. Scholtz would never leave his wife, the daughter of the publisher. Afterward, Tina kissed me on the cheek and thanked me for my sage advise.

Spring turned to summer and summer to fall and still nothing so I called Michalski. He still had nothing to tell me. He suggested I sell my condo and move. But I could not do that. I had not received a raise from that stingy rat Scholtz in ten years. I resolved to take my life into my own hands. How many years did it take for the government to find and kill Osama Bin Laden?

By then I was sure that Pedro tried to kill me. So what was good for the goose was good for the gander. I watched YouTube videos on how to make red velvet cupcakes. I practiced making them with plastic gloves, leaving no fingerprints. I bought rat poison at the hardware store.

I left a plastic plate full of red velvet cupcakes at his door, covered in plastic cellophane. A few days later, the police and the coroner were at his apartment. Yellow tape was draped across his door. "Police lines. Do not cross."

Inspector Michalski told me that Pedro had been killed by strychnine poisoning. He urged me to move from the building. He said a psychopathic killer was on the loose.

A few days later, the killer left another red velvet cupcake with red and blue balloons on white icing at my door. Inspector Michalski took the cupcake and dusted the area for fingerprints. The cupcake was laced with strychnine.

V.   The Funeral

I went to Pedro's funeral at the local Catholic Church. The priest spoke

kindly of him to the overflowing crowd. A teen-aged boy spoke how

Pedro Alvarez was like a father to him. Many people cried. Pedro's

American girlfriend "Kris" also spoke at his funeral. She told about

how they met at the local animal shelter, near the state penitentiary.

Pedro loved animals and often volunteered at the shelter and would

bake pastries for the shelter's fundraisers. She held his new puppy dog.

The service was mostly in Spanish. We followed the hearse to the

cemetery where Pedro was buried.

At the repast, a skinny teen-age boy balanced his plastic plate

on top of an overflowing trash can. He raised both arms. Touchdown!

There was all kind of Mexican foods: tamales, baked chicken

enchiladas and Mexican rice. They also had my favorite red velvet

cupcakes with cream cheese filling. Afterwards, I became depressed.

Given the fact I received another poisoned cupcake, it was clear I

poisoned the wrong person. Pedro was not the killer.

I changed my mind and accepted my sister Mavis's invitation for Thanksgiving dinner at her house in Los Angeles. I needed to get away. My older brother Lyndon and his family would be there. I can't stand him.

I boarded the last plane out of Dulles International to LAX, sitting next to this smelly fat guy who spilled over into my seat. Immediately after takeoff the chubalard fell asleep and snored. The guy sounded like the San Andreas Fault had finally shifted. His mouth opened and he drooled. Needless to say I did not get much sleep.

I am the only unmarried sibling in my family. Lyndon and Mavis think I am a loser. Lyndon is a school teacher and Mavis is married to a lawyer named Purvis. They think they are better people than they are.

Mavis picked me up at the airport in her newest black Mercedes SUV. She kissed me on the check and hugged me. "How are you big brother? You look a little run down. I'm worried about you."

"Oh, you know the same. How are you?"

"The boys and I just got back from a mini vacation. Purvis took us to Santa Barbara for the weekend. Do you like my tan?"

"Looks nice. At 45, you still are the hottest girl in LA."

"I know," she said fluffing her hair in the rear-view mirror.

"You're so conceited."

They both laughed. "I know," she said again.

"I was watching a YouTube video on narcissists," I said. "It really fits your personality."

"You think so?" she said, fluffing her hair some more and then tossing her head.

"So how are the kids?"

"As you know, Bob is getting his Ph.D. Shelly was just accepted at Harvard. They both worked so hard. We are so proud of them. You know, Purvis just won trial lawyer of the year for a second year in a row."

"How is Lyndon doing?"

"Teaching history," she said. "Coaching soccer. Last year, they won division but were knocked out in the first round of the playoffs. You know Lyndon"

"Yeah, do I know Lyndon. What a loudmouth loser."

"Be kind," she said. "You are a lot like him."

"How are his kids?"

"You know James is in his first year of law school. Junior, you know, is still trying to find himself. He was in another auto accident.

This time they took away his driver's license. Remember, you did not
hear this from me."

"Was he drinking again?"

"I don't know."

"Figures."

"And you?"

"You know. The church and charitable work keeps me pretty
busy. Everybody talks about how amazing and kind I am. What about
you Walter?"

"You know, still searching."

Mavis really rolled out the red carpet for Thanksgiving.
Turkey, stuffing, gravy, mashed potato, corn on the cob, crab salad,
buttermilk rolls and pumpkin pie.

Purvis said grace. Afterwards, he thanked Mavis and kissed
her on the cheek. There seemed something cold and formal about
them. Their hearts were not in it.

"Ah, remember the Thanksgivings we used to have," Lyndon
said. "I was always mom and dad's favorite. Remember when dad
made Walter finish his dinner in the garage that Thanksgiving. He was
so scared of spiders. Hahaha. Dad warned him not to take more than he

could eat. Remember dad used to say 'get what you eat and eat what you get.' Hahaha."

"No offense guys but my kids are the smartest of all," Lyndon said. Lyndon rose to his feet bumping the table. He noisily rummaged through the refrigerator and helped himself to another beer. Marvis looked knowingly at Purvis who quietly laughed. I pictured myself cramming an arsenic-laced red velvet cupcake down Lyndon's throat.

Lyndon spoke about how unfriendly his neighbors were and about the loss of community in our society. "We used to have great neighbors Our new neighbors are strangers. I invited our new neighbor – a Chinese guy – for lunch. He said he and his wife don't have time for those kinds of things."

He spoke about how stupid his students were. "One kid mixed up Mexico and Canada on a geography quiz and a second kid copied him." His wife seemed bored.

"Hey, Uncle Lyndon, how goes the soccer team?" Bob said, trying to change the subject.

"Yeah, Uncle Lyndon, are you going to win division again?" Shelly said.

"This year we are going all the way," Lyndon said. "It is all about discipline. When my kids become ineligible because of their grades I line them up at the goal and have the other kids shoot penalty kicks at them. It's the way dad would have done it.

"Say, Walter," Lyndon said, his eyes glowing with wicked satisfaction. "How's your love life going?" His wife kicked him under the table. I could see the white table cloth shake. "They say that if you let too much sperm build up in your body it clouds the brain." He laughed like crazy at his own joke.

"You know I'm kidding, don't you? I love you, Walter," he said. He stood up and helped himself to another beer.

The next night I took the red-eye flight back to Washington, DC. Mavis offered to drive me to the airport but I took an Uber. There is only so much of my family I can stomach.

When I left Mavis hugged me and Purvis shook my hand. "Don't listen to Lyndon," Purvis said. "He has a stunted personality."

"Don't be so judgmental with people," Mavis said. "If you want to only have perfect friends, you will have no friends at all. Same with family."

On my plane trip back home, I thought about who tried to kill me. It was that Nazi Hermann. He was an exterminator, right? He had a cold, cruel face. He probably gassed Jews during the war.

Poison could not be used this time. No, I had to do something else. I decided to quietly follow Hermann. I am great at being stealthy.

I watched Hermann from my window, noting the license plate number of his work van. I wore my fake mustache and shadowed him during my off time.

After work and on weeknights, he frequented a nudie bar. His favorite girl was Trixie. After the bouncer at the door checked my identification with his flashlight, I sat in the back of the club so Hermann would not notice me.

Hermann ate and drank beers with Trixie. When she danced on stage, he stood at the foot of the stage and generously tipped her. Trixie was beautiful but she had pink and blue spiky hair and earrings that pierced her nose and lips. Her music was electronic and when she danced she was not in sync with her music. Hermann looked like her grandfather.

The interior of the club was a dark garish red. Cherry, the stripper on stage, finished her dance to Jimi Hendrix's *Little Wing*, her naked figure swinging on a pole. She daintily put on her red and black lingerie on stage

As she got off stage, everyone clapped. The next stripper Carolina put a dollar into Cherry's garter belt and mounted the stage.

Afterwards, Cherry came to my table. I cracked a couple jokes. "Do you like Abraham Lincoln?"

"He's my favorite president," she said as she stretched open her red garter belt. She laughed and I tucked a five spot into her garter belt. She snapped it close on my fingers. She demurely smiled and then turned and waved to me before flying to the next table. I waited for 30 minutes after Hermann left before leaving myself.

As I passed the alley, he grabbed me and threw me against the brick wall. "Are you following me?" The dank, dark alley smelled of urine and rotting garbage.

"I don't know what you mean."

He tore off my fake mustache. "Why are you following me?

"I'm not."

"Yes, you are. You are the strange little man who lives in the apartment above me." He turned me around and twisted my arm behind my back.

"Ow . . ow . . . . ow."

"Why are you following me?" he panted, as the stench of his beer breath blew into my face. As he pushed me up against the brick wall of the building, he slipped on wet garbage in the alley and fell to the ground. I slipped away from his grip and punched him in the face, knocking him backward.

I pulled the .45 from my coat and shot him in the face and again in the side of his head as he lay sprawled on the ground. Blood spattered on my shoes. I ran for my life.

VI.   The Killer

I thought about Tina Bottoms. That wolf Schlotz was bold. I pretended

not to look but I watched them from the corner of my eye. Sometimes

he massaged her back at her cubicle. Other reporters gossiped about

her.

When Tina left the ladies' room, her eyes were red.

"What's the matter?" I asked.

"I trusted you," she angrily said.

"What do you mean?"

She burst into tears. "I was fired," she said.

"What? When?"

"Five minutes ago."

"That dirty Scholtz," I said.

"What am I going to do?" she asked. "What am I going to tell

my parents?"

"I'm shocked," I confessed. "I don't know what to say."

"At least he promised to help me get a new job," she said. "Some of his friends told me to send my resume. He would put in a good word for me."

"That prick."

"Stop," she said.

"I'm sorry," I said.

"Go away," she said. "This is none of your business."

She filled a box with her personal items –her files, her dictionary and her thesaurus. I carried her box to her car.

Tina stiffly stuck her hand out to me. I shook it.

"Walter, you are the only real friend I had here at the newspaper." She got in her car and left. I watched her car leave the parking lot and then disappear down the street.

That night I received another red velvet cupcake with red and blue balloons on white icing. Things were getting confusing. If the killer was not Pedro or Hermann, who could it be? I called Michalski. He came that night with forensic experts.

I sold my condo. I gave Scholz my two-week termination notice.

"Why?" he asked.

"I have my reasons," I said as I laughed at him. He glared back.

"Put it in writing, Faff," he said as he sprayed disinfectant in his hands and rubbed them together.

Michalski called me the next day. He told me Hermann Schmidt, the man downstairs, had been shot and killed. The murder along with the death of Pedro Alvarez was front-page news.

I turned down Michalski's suggestion to go into hiding.

At this point, I thought about my remaining neighbors. It could only be the Hetheringtons or Nora Smithfield, I resolved to kill them and then flee. I closed my bank accounts.

That night I went to the Hetherington's apartment with my tire iron in hand. I knocked on their door.

"Hello," Ethel said. "Who is it?"

"Delivery," I said, disguising my voice. The dead bolt clicked. She opened the door.

I pushed the door wider. "What do you want?" she demanded.

I struck her head with the tire iron and she fell backward, crashing to the floor.

She tried to crawl away on all fours. I hit her again and then again with the tire iron, cracking her skull.

"Ethel," her husband called. "Ethel, what is going on?"

I entered their bedroom. Dick's eyes grew wide. He tried to turn in his bed. I began hammering his head with the tire iron. There was blood all over his sheets and comforter.

Not taking any chances, I went to Nora's apartment and knocked on the door.

"Who is it," said a gruff voice from the other side of the door.

"Moo," I said.

She opened the door. I shoved against the door, breaking the chain lock. She was waiting with a drawn revolver. I hit her arm with the tire iron, knocking the gun from her hand. "I loved your cupcake," I said and then bludgeoned her to death.

I washed my hands, changed my bloody clothes and shoes and then fled in my car into the night. I left my cell phone at my apartment so I could not be tracked.

My bloody clothes, the rat poison and the tire iron were thrown into a dumpster behind the supermarket. I wondered for a moment, "What if it was another neighbor?"

VII. The Getaway

The newspapers said the police were trying to find me. I wore my fake mustache and used cash in all my transactions. My picture was on the front page. I was dubbed "The Red Velvet Cupcake Murderer."

I drove to a remote two-story motel in the mountains. I would stay there until things cooled down. It would give me time to think. A woman named Frances checked me in. She was a pretty no-nonsense woman with dark brown hair that fell down to her shoulders.

The motel and restaurant were owned by Frances. She lived there with her teen-aged son Aaron.

I rented a room on the upper floor. I could see the entire parking lot and the entrance from my window. My alias was "Gary Cooper."

The next day it snowed. I put on my mirrored sunglasses and fake mustache and went to the motel restaurant. I bought a newspaper from the stand outside the front door and then sat down to order. At the counter by the cash register, a glass displayed featured red velvet cupcakes.

"Good morning, Mr. Cooper," Frances cheerfully said from the kitchen. A waitress named Lily took my order. *Alone Again* played on the restaurant music track. Two other customers in the restaurant – an old married couple - both wore red "Make America Great Again" baseball caps. Aaron, Frances's son, sat a table doing his algebra homework. School was closed for the day because of the snow.

I ordered corned beef hash, two fried eggs sunny-side up and fried potatoes with coffee and orange juice. The paper said Donald Trump this and Donald Trump that. Donald Trump negotiating with Kim in Vietnam. Michael Cohen, his former lawyer, testifying on Capitol Hill. Wasn't there any other news? You turn on the news. That is all you hear. After I finished my breakfast, I read the newspaper. "A red velvet cupcake and more coffee," I said.

"How is it going, kiddo?" Frances asked her son.

"I just don't get this Algebra stuff," Aaron said.

"I'm sorry, I can't help you there," his mother said.

"Excuse me, perhaps I can be of assistance," I offered. "Algebra was a long time ago but I was good at it." I did get an A in the subject in junior high school.

We had a look at it. It was a plane problem. If plane X took off from LAX and flew to Chicago O'Hare airport at 400 mph and plane Y took off from Chicago O'Hare airport and flew to LAX airport when would they meet? Very logical. Once explained, Aaron caught on.

"You know mathematics is so important," I said. "It explains the universe."

We worked on his mathematics homework all morning and then his English composition assignment.

Aaron was the star of the high school basketball team. But he was in danger of losing his eligibility because of his poor grades.

I explained to Aaron the geometry of basketball. He arched his shot is because the hole of the basketball was larger for an arching shot than a flat shot. Aaron was impressed.

He asked if I would see his basketball game on Friday. I agreed.

I first watched the junior varsity game and then the varsity game. Aaron was absolutely magnificent. He scored twenty points, pulled down ten rebounds and blocked two shots. He was unstoppable.

When we got to the restaurant that night, it was still busy. Lily brought us steaks, baked potatoes and a chef salad.

"On the house," she said and smiled.

Lily brought Aaron a chocolate milkshake with whipped cream and a cherry on top. I shook my head. "You're in training," I said. "You know I saw Pistol Pete Maravich play against the Lakers in Los Angeles. You remind of Pistol Pete."

"Yes, Mr. Cooper," Aaron said. "Send it back, Lily."

"Mr. Cooper, you know so much."

"Aaron, I've been around. I know a thing or two."

"Yes."

Afterwards, Frances thanked me. "You know being a single mom is difficult. Fridays are the busiest nights for us. I have yet to see him play a game. Mr. Cooper, thank you for going to see my son play. It meant the world to him."

"Please, call me Gary," I said.

"Okay, Gary. Thank you."

Things were going great so it was inevitable that everything would come crashing down.

One early morning, I saw the SWAT team pull up. It was still dark but I could see them under the glow of the pink-orange street lights of the parking lot. I grabbed my coat and pistol and went to the motel office. It was snowing.

I woke up Frances and Aaron and took them hostage. The police sealed off the area and began evacuating the motel. I opened the curtain. Numerous state police cars and country sheriff cars had pulled up. I helicopter circle above.

"What is the meaning of this, Gary?"

"I'm not Gary," I said. "I'm Walter Faff."

"You are the man they are looking for in the news?"

"Yes. That's me."

Her mouth dropped open. Aaron began to cry.

"What are you going to do to us?" Aaron asked.

"You can do whatever you want to me but please let Aaron go," Frances said. "He has his whole life ahead of him."

"No one will get hurt if you cooperate," I said.

"Walter Faff," the police said over bullhorn. "This is the police. You are surrounded."

I saw police officers running into position through the curtain of the front office window.

"Walter Faff, give yourself up," he said.

A second police officer took the bullhorn. "Walter, this is Michalski. We don't want to harm you. Please surrender."

Both Frances and Aaron were now crying.

"Please Mr. Faff," Frances pleaded. "We know you are a good man."

The telephone rang. I picked up the telephone. It was Michalski.

"Walter, is everybody okay?" he said. I could hear running outside. "Are you okay?"

"Yes, I'm fine."

"Who is with you?"

"The owner of the motel and her son."

"Are they okay?"

"Yes, they are."

"There is someone here who wants to say something to you."

"Hello, Walter. This is Mavis." She was crying.

"Yes. Hello."

"Walter, please. This is not you."

I did not know what to say.

"Please give up and let those innocent people go."

I started to cry.

"Walter, please. I know you. You are a good man. There must be some kind of mistake."

"C'mon, Walter." It was Michalski again. "Let Frances and Aaron go and surrender. We don't want anyone hurt, including you."

After I surrendered, a SWAT team member violently tackled me from my blindside, causing me to fall face forward and breaking my front teeth on the concrete sidewalk. I tasted the blood from my split lip and myy face went numb. I felt the cold steel barrel of the police officer's pistol pressed against my head. Another police officer jerked my hands behind my back and handcuffed me. After they frisked me for weapons, they took me away. My arrest was on the news and in the newspapers.

All the media was at the show trial. They called it the red velvet cupcake murders, even though only one person died from being poisoned by a cupcake. Of course, Michalski accused me of poisoning myself to hide his own incompetence.

The prosecutor called me a monster for killing my neighbors. If Michalski and Smith had done their jobs to protect and serve the public I would not have killed anyone.

My lawyers hired an expert witness to testify that I was insane. I should not have agreed to it. The crazier you are, the more likely they are to lock you up. I did what I did to protect myself. After deliberating for as long as it takes for a hungry man to finish his meal, the jury unanimously found me guilty.

Here I am now alone on death row. I live in a concrete cell with a toilet. At mealtime, the prison guards shove my meals through a slot in the door. Every once in a while my lawyers come to see me. I exercise once a day in the yard. I read all I want. I have all the time in the world.

Mavis visited once. Lyndon apologized on the news to all the victims' families on behalf of our family. Bart Schlotz said in a television interview that he would never have suspected me of being a serial killer. "You never really know anybody," he said. They both seemed upright pillars of the community. I feel like Jesus Christ being crucified for all of mankind's sins.

My lawyers tell me they can tie up my execution for decades by appeals. I'm not going anywhere.

Not far from the state penitentiary, a gap tooth woman named Kris in her animal shelter uniform baked red velvet cupcakes with cream cheese filling for a fundraiser at the animal shelter. She painstakingly drew red and blue balloons with an icing bag on the white frosting of each cupcake.

A Better Life
By Mark Kodama

I. The Kitchen Mama

The sun has not risen yet. It is early morning at a house of prostitution in a small city in the southern part of the island of Honshu, Japan. The year is 1910. Shizuko, a beautiful woman in her late thirties, prepares breakfast. Her seventeen-year-old son, Minoru, opens the door. He is carrying cordwood for the kitchen stove. The morning is cold and both Shizuko and Minoru wear coats.

"Don't forget your mask," Shizuko says. "And here is your lunch."

"Mother, I have it," Minoru replies.

"Don't rush. Just take your time."

"Don't worry so much." Minoru says. "I will be home by afternoon."

"I really liked your drawings and new poems."

"Thank you, Mother," Minoru says.

"You are talented and getting better. Last night I dreamed that you were living in America and you were driving a grand, brand-new black shiny car with your pretty wife and two young daughters.

America, Minoru. Dream of it. Then make it happen. Minoru, find who you are. Once you find who you are, don't let anyone else define you. Paint your own canvas in life. Your life is your own and belongs to no one else."

Shizuko is washing rice in the kitchen. Steam from the first pot of rice is already rising from the black pot, bubbling over on the wood-burning stove. Shizuko adds sticks of wood to the fire.

She can feel someone looking at her. She gazes at the reflection in the window and sees Kodama the Elder standing in the kitchen doorway. He swallows hard as he looks upon the former beauty.

Yong Ran Pei, the beautiful prostitute, sits on the balcony of the second floor of the brothel and watches the people moving in the street. Her face is painted white and lips red. She sings as she combs her long black hair that falls on the front of her white silk kimonos.

On the street, Fujinaka, the blind bookkeeper, cocks his head as he listens to Yong Ran Pei's lilting voice. "She is just like Shizuko was," Fujinaka says to himself. "Same history. Same fate. Well, some things should be left unsaid."

II. The Shit Collector

Minoru pushes a wooden cart that rattles along the cobblestone street. People cover their noses and run from the stink. A man covering his nose with a cloth quickly hands Minoru a covered bucket then disappears into his building. Ryoji, the brothel owner's son, looks upon Minoru from the second balcony of the brothel. He is dressed in a suit and tie and wears a thin mustache. He stares down upon Minoru with sadness.

Minoru arrives at the farm of Matsumura the Mayor on the outskirts of the city. Matsamura is fifty with jet-black hair. He is clean shaven with a medium build. Minoru is selling bags of dried human waste to the farmers. He has big hands and a kind face.

"I have a question for you, Minoru san," Matsamura says. "I hope it does not offend you."

"Yes?"

"Why are you always so happy?" he asks. "This world is so full of sadness and injustice. And the bad are rewarded while the good suffer."

"Why do you think I am always happy when I wear a mask all the time?"

"I can tell by the way you walk–the way you move," the mayor replies. "And you are always singing such happy songs."

"I don't really know. It seems to me life is a gift and every day offers new presents."

"I like what you say," the mayor nods. "We will see you again next week. I would like to talk more with you."

—

"Why are you wasting your time and energy on Yong Ran Pei?" Shizuko asks her son. "Do you see this coat? Do you think it keeps you warm? No. That is only an illusion. It is the heat from your own body that keeps you warm. The coat only allows you to retain you own heat. Be like your body–the source of your own warmth."

"I'm not wasting my time," Minoru says.

"She is a prostitute, Minoru. She is not the kind of girl you marry. She is not even Japanese."

"I never said I would marry her," Minoru says.

"You don't have to say anything. I know you. I can see it in your eyes. The Chinese have a saying 'Don't play a musical instrument to a cow.'"

"What harm is there in it?"

"She will only bring you tears. Can't you see she sleeps with Kodama the Elder, Kodama the Younger, and the customers, all who have money. We don't have anything. See her new red silk kimono–a gift from Kodama the Younger. Her shiny new gold pendant–a gift from Kodama the Elder. What do you have to give her?

"Love."

"All your tears for someone incapable of love," his mother says. "Focus your efforts on improving yourself and you will find someone who will appreciate your gifts."

"Thoughts of Yong Ran Pei make me eager to get up each and every day."

"Youth is fleeting. The gifts will stop someday, then you will find you are just like everyone else. And then you will stop caring. People get older. Outer beauty is transient. Inner beauty is eternal. Dream of America. Taste it. Breathe it. When you get there, your past will not matter. You will be able to succeed on your own abilities. Prepare yourself and be bold when the moment comes. Be ready for opportunity when it presents itself. Success or failure in life turns on a few key moments."

"I will bring you with me," Minoru says. His mother looks beautiful again, like when she was twenty. She smiles as her breasts heave.

"No, Minoru. This is *your* dream. Maybe it could have been my dream once upon a time, but I am old, and my life is here.

"I will bring you with me."

"Yes, Minoru," Shikoku laughs, and Minoru's eyes light up. "I would like that. Some day we will climb to the top of the Statue of Liberty together. Now here is dinner for Kodama the Elder and Kodama the Younger. Please take them their meals."

Kodama the Elder enters the room. Kodama is small but strongly built. He is in his mid-forties but looks much younger and has jet black hair. "Hello, Shizuko and Minoru," he says kindly. "I hope I am not interrupting anything."

"Nothing important Kodama san," Shikoku says, her eyes looking down.

"I have more drawing paper and ink for your son," Kodama

the Elder announces. "Minoru is very talented. We are all so very proud

of him. And here is a book on Western paintings.

"Thank you, Uncle," Minoru says.

"I must be on my way," the brothel owner says. "I have

business to take care of. I will be back tonight. Study hard, Minoru."

Please take your meal before you go," Shikoku says. "Minoru,

serve Kodama san his meal. I prepared your favorite broiled salmon."

—

Matsumura the Mayor and Minoru stand outside the mayor's

farmhouse.

"I have the answer to your question, Matsumura san," Minoru

says.

"What question was that?" the mayor asks.

"The one you asked me last week."

"You mean about happiness?"

"Yes."

"What is the answer then?"

"I dream about America."

"How do you know about America?" the mayor asks.

"I read about it."

"I didn't know you could read."

"My mother taught me."

"Ah, the beautiful Shizuko. Who taught your mother how to read?"

"I don't know. I never thought about it."

"What a beautiful soul your mother has. She only thinks of you."

"America is the place where anyone can become president. You are only limited by your own limitations and the limits of your imagination."

"Ah, if only such a wonderful place existed, Minoru. The world is so full of pettiness and oppression."

Minoru points to the temple and smiles. "It does exist, and I will get there. To make great things happen you must dream them first.

Matsumura claps Minoru on the back. "Young man, I like the way you think. Dream, Minoru. Dream."

Suddenly, the two men hear a loud shriek. The mayor's wife runs toward them. "Ryoske, Bunni has fallen into the cesspool," she shouts in panic.

Both men run to the cesspool. Minoru, running ahead of the

mayor, jumps into the cesspool and pulls the child out of the sewage.

"Get clean water,' Minoru shouts.

The young man carries the child out of the pond. They go to the well. They wash the child. Minoru takes off his own filthy clothes and then he washes his body. The stench is unbearable. The mayor's wife brings a bowl of cold water for Minoru.

"Thank you, Minoru san," the mayor's wife says, tears in her eyes.

"Yes. Minoru san," the mayor adds. "We owe our lives to you."

Minoru bows his head.

"A thousand thanks to you," the mayor's wife says.

"I will bring you some new clothes," the mayor says. "You can wear my clothes."

"Please wash my clothes," Minoru replies. "I will wear them when they are dry. You are too kind to me."

"You will wear my clothes," the mayor insists. "I will tell Kodama san about this. His family once lived here as samurai family. What can I do for you, Minoru san?

"Nothing. What I did was nothing."

"You are too humble."

"Yes, Matsumura san."

"What do you really want? Please tell me."

"Nothing, really."

"You must want something."

Minoru hesitates and then replies. "I want to learn how to ride a horse and shoot a gun like a samurai."

"I will teach you myself," Mastumura says.

III. The Prostitute

Minoru sits stoically, cross legged, on the wood floor outside the room of the prostitute Yong Ran Pei. Laughter from a young man and the woman emanate from the room. The man calls to Minoru from the room. It is the owner's son, Kodama the Younger. He is short, slight, with a thin pencil mustache. Kodama, dressed in a colorful blue and white cloth kimono, sits upon a silk cushion behind a low cherry wood table, drinking sake from a black and red lacquer bowl.

"Minoru, fetch the red kimono in my room and bring it here."

"Yes, Kodama san," he says, eyes downcast. "Right away."

Minoru leaves and then returns quickly with the beautiful red silk kimono. "May I enter the room."

"Yes, come in," Kodama the Younger says as he eyes the young prostitute, Yong Ran Pei, who is sitting next to Kodama. She is half naked, her kimono covering her hips. Her silken hair half covers her firm young breasts.

"You see my darling, I am a man who knows few words," Kodama the Younger says, imperiously lifting his bowl of sake. "But I am a man of action."

Kodama the Younger gives the expensive silk kimono to Yong Ran Pei. She squeals with delight, flashing an exquisite smile.

"This is beautiful," she says, feigning surprise. Although she is young, she is accustomed to receiving gifts from wealthy men. "Thank you Kodama san."

Kodama the Younger, noticing Minoru was still in the room, says curtly, "Fool, what are you doing still standing here like a country bumpkin? Can't you see we are having a private moment? Wait outside."

Minoru bows his head and returns to his place outside the room.

—

Minoru is lying in a flat bed with the beautiful Korean prostitute, Yong Ran Pei. Her gold pendant around her neck dances as she moves. Yong Ran Pei rises and folds her red kimono before placing it on a pile of other kimonos.

"You are beautiful," Minoru says, his eyes sparkling.

"I know," she says and laughs.

"I love you," Minoru says.

She looks at him for a moment. Her large dark eyes melting. She heaves a sigh. "I know."

"I have something for you," Minoru says, as Yong Ran Pei places her kimonos in the closet with her other gifts.

"What is it?"

"You must turn your back."

"What kind of present?

Minoru motions for her to turn her back. He hands her a package wrapped in light red paper and tied with a dark red ribbon. She opens the present. It is a poem with a drawing on it. She is delighted.

"You know I can't read. Read it to me."

They both sit up on the mat on the floor. Yong Ran Pei smiles at him.

Minoru recites his haiku.

"Your white knight is here,

Not atop a great war steed,

But walking on foot."

"Someday I will marry you and take you to America."

"Aiyo!" she says. "You are such a dreamer. And what makes you think I would like to go to America?"

"Because in an America even a poor man can own a mansion, wear the finest clothes, and eat steak every night.

"You talk too much.

"I just say what is in my heart."

"Minoru, you can't change your fate. Your fate is decided by the gods."

"You *can* change your fate. If you let other lesser people define your dreams, then your fate will be decided. Life is a canvas. And the canvas is blank. You must paint your own canvas with your own dreams."

"What makes you so restless?"

"Sometimes I feel like I am buried alive in a tomb. I either have to break free or kill myself.

"Minoru, you are a good boy but poor and from a poor family. Have you considered that I may have dreams of my own?"

"We are poor but why should we live in cages built by others. What are your dreams? Define yourself. Do you love me?"

"I don't love anyone. I don't believe in love.

"If you do not love anyone, including yourself, then how can anyone love you? Sometimes, love is all we have."

"I don't like you when you are like this, Minoru. Talk, talk, talk. It gives me a headache.

"Do you love me?"

She looks away. "No. You are a poor boy."

"I ask again: do you love me?"

"Sometimes, I love you."

—

"You are a good boy, Minoru," Fujinaka the blind bookkeeper says. "But someday you will learn the natural order of things. It is better you learn this sooner rather than later. The gods distain the impertinent.

"Alexander was king of Epirus. In Epirus, the River Acheron flowed. It was foretold that Alexander would die at the River Acheron. So, when Alexander invaded Italy with his mighty army he was sure of his success for he knew he would die at the River Acheron in Greece.

"When Alexander was crossing a river in Italy, the enemy appeared in great numbers. When Alexander asked his Italian companions what was the name of the river, they told him Acheron. Alexander then charged the enemy and died a noble death. You see, Minoru, even kings cannot escape their fate."

"Did my mother speak to you?"

"Yes of course. She is concerned about you. She has enough worries, don't you think? Life is difficult and not always fair. You must learn to endure."

"Yes. Uncle. You are right about everything."

"You must know your place. The Matsumuras ruled this community with the Kodamas sitting at their right hand. The Kodamas became too arrogant and fell from grace. They did not know their place. The nail that sticks up gets hammered down."

"Yes, uncle."

"Men who do not know how to live by the rules are men on their own. They are outlaws, animals, not fit to live in a society of men. Let me tell you the story about the monkey god. The monkey god was talented but undisciplined. The monkey god became so power hungry that he challenged the king of the gods himself for hegemony over the universe. Finally, the king of gods put a mountain on top of the monkey god, imprisoning the monkey god for a thousand years in granite. Grass bends and is eternal. But even the hardest stone gets worn down by rushing water and is washed away to the sea. Know your place. You cannot change your destiny."

IV. The Mayor

Mayor Matsumura invites Minoru to join him and his men to buy horses in Kyoto.

"I must ask Kodama san," Minoru says.

"I spoke with him already. It has all been arranged. I have a gun and a horse for you. We leave on Saturday. Be here at dawn." The mayor gives Minoru and handful of coins. "This is for you."

"Thank you," Minoru says. "I will give them to my master."

"Kodama san has been paid. These are for you, my young friend. When I look into them, I can see a thousand things going on behind your eyes. I see a great future for you, Minoru. Greatness can come from anywhere, even from the most humble."

—

Matsumura and his entourage pass through Rashomon Gate, and enter into the ancient capital. Nicha, a Buddhist monk, dressed in saffron robes, preaches to a hostile crowd that has gathered at the market to watch a tightrope walker cross a high wire strung across two temple towers.

"Friends. I herald the coming of the higher man.," the monk says. "God is dead. There is only beast and man. Rise above the common man, the herd. Live the life of the higher man. There is only beast and man. I am the monk, Nicha, from Nagasaki, the city of the Christian martyrs. I've come down from the mountains to save you. There are no sinners; no saints. There is no afterlife. Rise above the common man. Rely upon yourselves for your own salvation. I love followers who are leaders and leaders who follow. I love those who love to think and think to love. I love those who know their own limits and know that there are no limits. I love those who hate me and hate those who love me. I love those who fly free to be devoured by those who are caged. I herald the higher man who will smash the tablets of morality and create a new set of values."

"We have heard enough of this," a voice from the crowd calls out. "We want to see the tightrope walker."

"You have evolved from worms to man," the monk says. "Yet you still are worms. Man laughs at apes. Similarly, the higher man laughs at the common man. I see you laughing at me. Such icy laughter."

The tightrope walker emerges from one of the temple towers. He proceeds to cross the tight rope. When he reaches the half-way point, a jester emerges from the same tower.

"Out of my way," the jester says. "Make way for your better."

The jester jumps over the tightrope walker, causing him to lose his balance and fall to the ground, arms flailing in the air. The crowd gasps and scatters as the tightrope walker falls to his death.

The monk quietly speaks to the dying tightrope walker. The monk then hoists the corpse of the tightrope walker over his shoulder and walks through the parting crowd toward Rashomon Gate.

Matsumura turns to Minoru. "Everything is always before us. Some people see it and others don't."

—

Matsumura, two of his men, and Minoru ride their horses on their return trip from Kyoto. Matsumura's men hold the reins of four additional horses that Matsumura bought in Kyoto. They arrive at a clearing at the end of the cedar forest. There is a small cemetery to the right of the men. The freshly dug graves house the bodies of the soldiers who died in the recently concluded Russo-Japanese War.

In the clearing at the crossroad, four bandits armed with

carbines and dressed in tattered Army uniforms approach. The leader wears a back patch over his left eye. The left side of his face appears to be half melted. He has a withered left arm and he walks with a limp. He brandishes a pistol in his right hand.

"We are revenue collectors," the bandit leader announces.

"For which town?" Mayor Matsumura asks. "I may know your mayor."

"Is it not enough that we just say it?" the bandit says.

"What do you say we owe?" the mayor inquires.

"What do you have? Never mind. I will check for myself."

"Stop where you are," the mayor says through clenched teeth. "We are not going to give you anything. If you take another step you are a dead man."

Minoru thinks that if he were the bandits he would put someone behind them. Since they are evenly matched there must be a reason why they are so bold. He looks at the tree behind to the right and sees a pair of feet dangling from the branches.

"We are not looking for trouble," the bandit chief says.

"Neither are we," the mayor replies. "Step aside."

"As you wish."

The bandit then turns his back and starts to walk away. He

spins suddenly, drawing a handgun. Without hesitation, Minoru shoots him in the chest. Matsumura shoots and wounds a second bandit who turns and runs.

Minoru then turns and shoots the bandit lurking in the tree. The man falls and hits the bushes.

One of Matsumura's men shoots a fourth bandit who attempts to flee. A fifth bandit escapes unharmed.

Minoru dismounts his horse. He approaches the mortally wounded bandit leader who is crawling toward the cemetery. Minoru then shoots the man in the back his head.

"Good work young Minoru," the mayor says. The mayor throws him a white cloth handkerchief. "I was thinking the same thing. Wipe the blood from your face and hands. I thought they had a man behind us. I just couldn't see him. You are a young man of talent. A man of talent is always useful."

"Thank you, Matsumura san. You are too kind."

"Here. Take this horse. It is my gift to you."

V. The Brothel Owner

Kodama the Elder, Kodama the Younger, and Minoru stand together beneath the balcony of the brothel. Kodama the Elder and Minoru talk as Kodama the Younger stands stoically with them, eyes downcast.

"I am very proud of you Minoru," Kodama the Elder says and smiles. "You are a man. Matsumura san has told me all you have done. Be patient. I have my own plans for you."

"Thank you, Uncle. I am not worthy of your honor."

—

Kodama the Younger and the bouncer, Nomi, wait at the stable next to the brothel as Minoru approaches.

"You are a shit collector, Minoru. Nothing more. That is all you are. That is all you will ever be. I am from a samurai family. If we had not suffered such reversals, we would still be with Matsumura and you and your mother would be on the streets. That horse is mine. We own you. We own your mother. You are our servant. Everything that you own belongs to us."

"I am sorry, Kodama san, but you are mistaken," Minoru says, eyes downcast. "Matsumura san gave the horse to me for killing the bandits. He taught me how to ride and shoot a gun. If anything is unclear, Matsumura san can clarify it.

"There is nothing to clarify. It is you who is mistaken. The beast is mine. The girl is mine, too. You know your poem? It made great toilet paper."

"It is not surprising that you would think that is what it is for."

"You are very womanish. Poems. Drawings. You are a woman!"

"The horse is mine, Kodama san."

"You will pay for your insolence. Nomi grab him.

The large bouncer grabs Minoru from behind then ties him up, wrapping a rope around his arms. He then forces Minoru down on his knees. Nomi forces Minoru's right hand onto a stone. With the side of a steel ax, Kodama the Younger smashes the hand. Minoru screams in pain.

Kodama the Elder and Fujinaka the blind bookkeeper enter the stable.

"What is this?" Kodama the Elder asks.

"My God!" Fujinaka says.

Kodama the Younger and Nomi quickly stand at attention. They look at the ground.

"Send for the doctor," Kodama the Elder tells the bookkeeper. Kodama the Elder, his face red, looks up a Nomi who is a head taller than him. The bouncer trembles. Kodama cuffs him, knocking him to the ground. "You have five minutes to pack your belongings and leave," he tells the bouncer.

"Papa san, the horse is ours," Kodama the Younger says.

"That is for me alone to say. Did you break Minoru's hand?"

Kodama the Elder picks up the ax and raises it up to the light.

"I hit Minoru with the ax, Papa san," Kodama the Younger says, eyes downcast. Kodama the Elder slaps Kodama the Younger in the face and then punches him in the stomach. He grabs him by the hair and punches him in the face again.

"Papa san, Nomi is not responsible. He was doing as I told him."

"Each man is responsible for his own action." Kodama the Elder turns to Minoru. "Let me see you hand."

"Papa san, I take full responsibility," Kodama the Younger says.

"You are lucky that I don't crush your hand. Idiot! Get out of my sight."

—

Kodama the Elder and Fujinaka are together on the street below the brothel. "This won't happen again. I'm going to hit them where it hurts. They will not fight anymore."

"What are you going to do?" Fujinaka asks.

"What I must do."

———

Minoru returns to see Yong Ran Pei but she is gone. Kodama the Elder, Kodama the Younger, and Minoru's mother are there to greet him. Minoru's right hand is bandaged.

"Control your anger," Shizuko says. "No more violence. Violence never satisfies anger. It only feeds a greater appetite for more anger."

"You boys are not to fight like that again," Kodama the Elder says.

"I did nothing," Minoru insists.

"Put it all behind you," his mother says.

"It does not matter," Kodama the Elder says. "She's gone. I sold her. There is nothing to fight about any more.

"Do you mean the horse?"

"No, the girl," Kodama the Elder says.

"Not Yong Ran Pei."

"Now do you see what you've done?" Kodama the Younger says. He is furious.

"Be quiet," Kodama the Elder says.

"She is all I have," Minoru says.

"And you did not really have her either," Kodama the Younger taunts. "We owned her, too."

"I told you to keep quiet," Kodama the Elder growls.

"Your mother is my father's concubine," Kodama the Younger says. "She warms his bed at night and warms his meals during the day. And you are our servant."

Minoru, enraged, rushes Kodama the Younger and knocks him backward out the second story window. Kodama the Younger breaks his neck and dies instantly.

The elder Kodama charges at Minoru. He punches him and then retrieves a knife. Minoru kicks him in the groin. Minoru runs to his room and grabs in pistol. With his left hand he shoots Kodama the Elder in the chest. Minoru then shoots the groaning Kodama in head.

Minoru turns to his mother who has witnessed the events. Her mouth is agape and tears run down her cheeks.

"What have you done?" she asks. "You must go now. Go to the mayor. He is a good man and will help you."

"Come with me," Minoru says.

"No, this is my home," his mother replies. She turns to one of the prostitutes "Send for the police and the doctor." Turning to a second prostitute, she says,"Call Fujinaka, the bookkeeper."

She turns to her son. "Go. I will see you in the next life. America, Minoru. Go to America, the land where dreams come true. Go quickly."

Minoru turns and runs out the brothel. He goes to the stable, mounts his horse, and rides to the mayor's farm.

—

"You must leave quickly," the mayor says. "Here is some food and money to get you to Osaka. Fujinaka has arranged for you to work as a sailor on a merchant ship called *The Phoenix,* bound for America. Meet him at the old inn."

"Thank you, Matsumura san."

"No time for thanks. You must go quickly. If you are caught, I never saw you."

"Goodbye, uncle. Thanks for everything."

"I hope you find your dreams in America. I think you will succeed. You are a capable young man. Now, go."

—

"Now that we are safely about the train, I must tell you something terrible that has happened," Fujinaka says.

Minoru is silent, still thinking of what had just happened. He looks up with vacant eyes.

"I did not want to tell you earlier because I did not want to impede your escape," the bookkeeper says.

"What can be worse than what has already happened?

Fujinaka is silent for a moment, reluctant to further hurt the sensitive young man, but at the same time eager to unburden himself of his secret. "Your mother is dead."

Minoru stares back in silence.

"She hung herself shortly after you left."

"My God! Am I responsible, Fujinaka san?"

"It is complicated. You must judge for yourself. I will also tell you who your father is."

"Is he alive?"

"He was ... until you killed him. Kodama the Elder was your father and Kodama the Younger was your half-brother. Your mother was his favorite prostitute. She was very intelligent and so he hired tutors to secretly educate her. After his wife died giving birth to Kodama the Younger, he asked your mother to marry him but she refused.

"My God. How could I be so blind?"

"The Kodamas had always protected the unprotected. That is why the clan had a falling out with the Matsumuras. A powerful member of the Matsumura clan raped a prostitute, so a Kodama killed him. At first the Kodamas protected the prostitutes and then they started running the brothels. Soon they became dependent on the trade. Your father was an uneducated man but someone who appreciated the value of education and who always did his best to be a just man.

"Your father loved you, too. He had you sell dung to the farmers and then held the money in trust for you. When you get to Seattle, you need to swim ashore. The captain will report you dead. Find the Waterfront Hotel. More money will await you there. I have friends there, you see."

"My God."

"As far as your brother, he was a good boy. He was just so jealous of you."

"Jealous of me? I have nothing."

"He had no mother to look out for him. And what kind of

talent did he really have?"

"All I know is that he hated me."

"You need to be able to walk in another's shoes to really understand them. There is no time to dwell on it. We've got to get to Osaka. *The Phoenix* leaves port in two days for Seattle. Put all this behind you. It was your mother's dream to give you a new life. There was only oppression for you here, Minoru. You are a very capable young man. Seek your fortunes in America. I lived in America for ten years. It may not be the country you think it is. But nothing is for free in this world. And that which is hard earned is more valuable than that which is given to you for free."

"Do you know where Young Ran Pei is?"

"Yes. But I will not tell you. All these people have died so you can now live. Minoru, make the most of your life. The gods control everything. The gods say people cannot escape their fates. But maybe you can. Good luck Minoru."

—

Minoru is naked on the deck of the ship in Puget Sound. It is pitch black on a moonless night. He holds a small bundle of clothes and shoes in his left hand.

"Death or a new life," Minoru says.

He then jumps from the deck of the ship into the frigid water of Puget Sound and swims for land. The small bundle of clothes is tied to his head.

Made in the
USA
Columbia, SC